She was seized by unbearable jealousy

For there, framed in the passageway backstage, was the man she loved, kissing his glamorous and talented co-star–the beautiful Suzanne Thomas.

"Oh, Nick, we ought always to be together!" she heard the lovely singer whisper fervently to Nicholas.

Stunned as if from a physical blow, Mary turned and rushed blindly from the scene, her mind chastizing herself for being such a fool...

...and her heart shattering into a thousand pieces.

D1115313

The Warrender Saga

Follow the famous conductor Oscar Warrender—and Anthea, his lovely opera-star wife—down the years in these delightfully entertaining novels. Each volume is a heartwarming romance set against the exciting background of opera or theater.

MARY BURCHELL

Unbidden Melody

Originally published as Harlequin Romance #1767

Harlequin Books

TORONTO · LONDON · NEW YORK · AMSTERDAM
SYDNEY · HAMBURG · PARIS

Original hardcover edition published in 1973
by Mills & Boon Limited

ISBN 0-373-01767-7

First Harlequin edition published March 1974

Second printing February 1977

The Warrender Saga, published October 1978

Printed in Canada

CHAPTER I

"THERE's only one thing for it," Dermot Deane informed his secretary, without looking up from his crowded desk. "*You* will have to go to the airport and meet Nicholas Brenner."

"*I* shall?" Mary did look up, and with a startled glance. "But —"

"Don't say 'but'," interrupted her employer irritably. "There is no sillier or flabbier word in the English language. I don't permit it in this office. Is that understood?"

"Yes, Mr. Deane," said Mary submissively.

Dermot Deane ran his hands through his thinning hair.

"I can deal with an emergency single-handed. Even a crisis, if necessary. But —" he stopped, coughed and changed that to "however" before Mary could quite suppress a smile — "However, when it comes to a catastrophe I expect co-operation, even if you are as raw as an egg and haven't been here three weeks. In any case, it was you yourself who suggested the man," he added, as though that clinched the matter.

In this he was literally correct, Mary had to admit. But then, if singers were being discussed at all, Nicholas Brenner was the first name which inevitably sprang to her mind.

Until she had come to work for Dermot Deane. Mary

Barlow had only occasionally glimpsed that much-tried, but highly successful, impresario in concert hall or opera house when one or other of his famous clients happened to be singing, playing or conducting. She had always thought of him – if she thought of him at all – as a stout, knowledgeable, imperturbable man, quite impervious to the winds of crisis, temperament or fickle chance which were part of his particular world. But when she came to replace his invaluable secretary of ten years' standing she discovered this was far from the case.

"He's just as temperamental as any of his clients," the departing Miss Evans informed her. "And usually with much more reason. He's the one who takes the final rap – the financial rap – if anything goes wrong. But all the time he has to look as though everything is going splendidly. *He* can't indulge in displays of nerves or temper. He's got to have the answer to everyone else's questions. No wonder agents and impresarios get ulcers!"

"Has he got ulcers?" Mary had enquired with sympathy.

Miss Evans said – not to her knowledge, but that was because for all these years he had had a good secretary who had taken half the load.

She was obviously referring to herself and at the same time giving Mary a hint that she must strive to follow worthily in her footsteps. So Mary made sympathetic noises to indicate that she would do her best.

"D.D. is pretty fair as bosses go," Miss Evans went on. "But if he turns savage, remember it probably just means that Torelli has been impossible, or Warrender unreasonable, or some indispensable tenor has inconsiderately gone and broken a leg or something."

Mary nodded her fair head gravely and promised to

remember. And she tried hard during the few days in which Miss Evans lingered to teach her her job, to absorb all she could of that lady's tough wisdom as well as her official expertise.

To Mary the position as Dermot Deane's secretary represented not only a promotion. It was in some ways the realisation of a dream. For as long as she could remember she had been fascinated by the world of music and musicians. But because, along with her essentially artistic outlook, there went a strong streak of realism, she accepted quite early in life the fact that intense musicality, a faultless ear, a degree of natural taste, and a small, pleasing voice did not add up to the necessary equipment for a real career in the musical world.

Fortunately, her parents – although they loved her dearly – also had no inflated ideas about their child's talents. Consequently, though they allowed her to cultivate her modest gifts for her own pleasure, they also saw to it that she was firmly equipped to earn her own living in a more conventional way. It is doubtful if the most devoted of parents can do more for their children.

As a result, Mary was spared the frustrating years of artificial hopes leading to inevitable disillusionment which are the lot of those who measure their ambitions by their wishes rather than a frank appraisal of their qualifications. At twenty-two she was an excellent secretary, with a working knowledge of two foreign languages. In addition she enjoyed a degree of self-respect which automatically forbade her to give less than good value for whatever salary she drew.

Instead of becoming an indifferent performer in her working hours, Mary became a pretty knowledgeable member of the audience when off duty – a position from which a great deal of enjoyment can be derived, and with which she would possibly have remained quite satisfied had she not heard of the pending vacancy in Dermot Deane's office.

She heard of this by way of the grapevine in the opera queue where she was booking tickets. And the moment her tickets were in her hand she rushed along to the office of Dermot Deane.

Something in the firm but modest way she stated her qualifications and enthusiasm must have impressed him – and even Miss Evans, so far as she was capable of being impressed by any successor – for he hardly hesitated at all about engaging Mary. He jibbed slightly when she said she must work out a month's notice with her present employers, but yielded immediately when she pointed out that if she were prepared to let them down, the day would come when she would probably let him down.

"All right," he agreed. And he persuaded Miss Evans to put off her pending retirement for a few weeks longer, until Mary could honourably forsake the quiet backwaters of her legal office to plunge into the exciting, turbulent, sometimes dark currents which coursed through the office of London's leading impresario.

It was on her third day that one of the crises to which Miss Evans has so prophetically referred occurred in almost classic detail. The tenor cast for some much-heralded performances of "Carmen" at the Opera House did inconsiderately break an arm, and Dermot Deane was approached to find a substitute of comparable reputation and attainments.

Mary was entranced by the discussion which then ensued. Well-known names flew to and fro between Dermot Deane and Miss Evans, names which, until then, had simply represented dazzling figures behind the footlights to her. But each one was considered, assessed and for one good reason or another discarded.

It was then that she looked up from her typewriter and suggested diffidently, "What about Nicholas Brenner?"

"What about him?" countered her employer with some irony.

"Wouldn't he do?"

"The top man will always 'do'," Dermot Deane informed her drily. "But as a stand-in for someone else —" he shook his head without completing the sentence. "Anyway, he's been out of circulation since that car crash last March."

"He wasn't much hurt himself," Miss Evans put in. "He must have recovered long ago."

"But he hasn't sung since. I suppose it's some sort of nervous reaction after his wife was killed, and these things are harder to deal with than anything else in an artist. All the same —"

He paused once more. And Mary, reluctant to abandon even a slight hope of securing the singer who was to her of all singers the most fascinating and splendid, tried again.

"Might he not be more willing to step in at a moment's notice than work himself up to a formal comeback?" she suggested.

"Could be." Dermot Deane looked reflective. "He isn't a difficult chap, really. As tenors go, of course," he added in parenthesis. "And Don José is one of his best roles. He might also be interested in Lensky, when they revive 'Eugene Onegin'. That would give —" he began to scribble on the side of his blotter. "M-yes. Eight performances. Perhaps ten. And Lensky isn't a killer role. Just a walk-over for a man like Brenner."

"He should make a good Lensky. He has excellent legs," observed Miss Evans unemotionally.

"It's his larynx, not his legs, that a tenor has to worry about," growled Dermot Deane.

"Good legs help too," Miss Evans insisted. "Particularly in that costume."

"And his Russian should be all right," Mary contributed eagerly. "He had a Russian grandmother, hadn't he?"

"They all have Russian grandmothers or Hungarian uncles or Spanish girl-friends if they think that will help," Dermot Deane said cynically. "But yes, Brenner's Russian is fluent. I remember hearing him once do the Idiot in 'Boris'. He was the Idiot to end all Idiots." And he went into a smiling trance at the recollection.

This was not quite the way Mary would have chosen to have her favourite tenor described, and she winced slightly at this slur on his romantic charm. But she said eagerly, "Then you'll try for him?"

"Yes, we'll try for him," Dermot Deane agreed, and he reached for the telephone.

There followed an exciting day or two of cables, long-distance telephone calls and express letters – typed by Mary with thrilling realisation that she was at the centre of a gorgeous operatic crisis. And, after Nicholas Brenner had finally been located at his lakeside hideout in Austria, the arrangements were made with remarkable smoothness and speed.

He was prepared, it seemed, to come back to the operatic world to play Don José in "Carmen" and Lensky in "Eugene Onegin". And the suggestion had been Mary's in the first place! As she typed the final contract, she felt

10

there were certain triumphs in the world of the theatre unmarked by applause or the sweeping up and down of curtains.

Dermot Deane was generous enough to permit himself an occasional genial, teasing reminder to Mary that it was she who had started the ball rolling. And this subtly flattered and pleased her. Until the morning when her employer – now bereft of the services of Miss Evans, and himself forced to fly to Paris to see Gina Torelli – informed Mary that she must go to London Airport to meet Nicholas Brenner in person.

"You can drive out with me in the Bentley," Dermot Deane informed her. "I have to go in half an hour. My plane takes off about ten minutes before Brenner's comes in. You wait for him and give him the V.I.P. treatment, and Carter will drive you both back into town."

Mary wanted to ask what the V.I.P. treatment consisted of. But, reminding herself that her employer had plenty of worries without having to cross all the "t's" and dot all the "i's" for her, she bravely forbore. She simply said, "Very well," with more composure than she felt.

"Here is his schedule of rehearsals and performances." Her employer handed her a sheaf of papers. "If he's running true to tenor form he's probably lost his copy by now. And tell him we've reserved his usual suite at the Gloria. They like that sort of little attention."

Mary took the proffered papers and put them in her briefcase. Half an hour later she and her employer left the office to drive to London Airport, Dermot Deane sitting in front perusing some papers and Mary behind, indulging in her own thoughts.

At no time in her carefree years as an opera fan could she have imagined herself actually having Nicholas Bren-

11

ner put in her care. The nearest she had ever got to him was to stand at the stage door after a performance and watch him come out, usually accompanied by his very beautiful wife – the woman who had been killed in the car crash last March.

Mary remembered her very well that last time, standing there framed in the stage door, her honey-coloured hair almost the same shade as the golden dress which clung to her like a sheath to an exotic flower. She had been laughing at the enthusiastic scene, and if ever a girl looked carefree and on top of the world that girl had been Monica Brenner.

Mary saw off her employer and then went to the arrival lounge to await Nicholas Brenner.

His plane was fifteen minutes late. Which gave her time to experience several waves of panic and fight these down as best she could. Like all inexperienced people – and in this particular respect she was inexperienced – she thought of a dozen mistakes which she might inadvertently be making. Was she really waiting in the right place? Should she be warm and friendly when he arrived? distant and respectful? talkative or silent? Did she look ridiculously young and inexperienced to be taking a famous tenor under her wing?

When he finally came, that seemed to be the first thing which struck him.

She went forward to greet the unmistakable figure, and the slightly nervous words which came out were, "Mr. Deane asked me to come and fetch you, Mr. Brenner. He had to go to Paris himself and –"

"You look rather small and young to be 'fetching' me," he observed with a very slight smile. "Did I need fetching?"

12

"Mr. Deane seemed to think so," she smiled.

"Felt I was not to be trusted to drive myself into town, I suppose?" There was a touch of nervous bitterness about that which she found terribly disconcerting.

"Maybe he was thinking more of me – and what a tremendous thrill it would be to be allowed to fetch – to meet you," she said calmly.

And at that his tense expression relaxed. He put his hand round her arm suddenly and said, "Come along then. Where is the car?"

He made a slight sign to the hovering porter, and they went out to the car, where the imperturbable Carter stepped out, saluted and said, " 'Morning, Mr. Brenner. Will you sit in front, or behind with Miss Barlow?"

"Behind, with Miss Barlow."

So the sumptuous-looking luggage was stowed away and they got into the car. And as they drove away Mary thought, "I'm sitting beside Nicholas Brenner!"

Nothing in her quiet, self-controlled manner betrayed what she was thinking. She gave him the papers which her employer had committed to her care, and as he studied them she remained silent. It was he who spoke first, and he did so without looking up from the papers.

"Why did you say it was a thrill to fetch me? Aren't you quite used to running around after Deane's clients?"

"Oh, no. I haven't been in his office three weeks," she explained with almost naïve candour. "You're the first star I've had to – to look after."

"You're doing quite well for a beginner," he told her, still without looking up, but she thought he sounded amused.

"It's not too easy to transform oneself from a fan into

13

a responsible representative of the firm," she informed him.

"No, I can imagine it has its difficulties," he agreed, so seriously that she *knew* he was amused. "So you are a fan? an operatic fan, I take it?"

"Yes. But —" she was afraid this was all beginning to sound rather too naïve and artless — "not the kind that mills round the stage door screaming."

"Don't you mill round the stage door?"

"Yes. But I don't scream."

He laughed at that — a short laugh, but he did laugh. And then he looked up at her at last, and she thought he was slightly surprised to find that he *had* laughed.

"May I hope that you have stood at the stage door for me in your time?"

"Oh, certainly. I've also cheered for you from the gallery."

"Thank you," he said. Then he lapsed into silence and looked out of the window.

She allowed herself one quick glance before she turned to look out of *her* window, and she was surprised to find how clearly his whole appearance was instantly impressed on her vision. He was a bigger man than she had realised. Not only tall, but wide in the shoulders with that total impression of over-life-size which belongs to almost all great stage artists.

From those stage-door glimpses she had not thought of him as having a slightly melancholy cast of countenance. Now he undoubtedly had. And because she thought he might be glad of something other than his own thoughts on the occasion of his first return to London, she said presently, "Mr. Deane had to go to Paris to see Madame Torelli."

14

"Oh – Torelli?" He turned immediately, with an expression of half-amused interest. "How is she?"

"Marvellously well. Is she ever anything else?"

"No. That incredible stamina and vitality! They're as breathtaking as her voice. I never knew anyone else with such staying power. Monica – my wife – used to say –" He stopped suddenly, as though he had forgotten how that sentence finished.

"Mr. Deane says it's her peasant stock," observed Mary smoothly, as though no break had occurred in the conversation.

"Yes, that's it," he agreed, as though snatching that moment for complete recovery. "A streak of the peasant – something really earthy – stands us all in good stead. I'm always glad of my good dash of peasant stock."

"Was that the Russian grandmother?" Mary asked with interest.

"Yes." He smiled a little. "How did you know?"

"I read an article about you once. It said you had a Russian grandmother. Did you know her?"

"Oh, yes!" Suddenly he looked genuinely interested, and like a different person. "She was a singer too in her youth. Not a top-liner, but she sang small parts with people like Sobinoff and Neshdanova –"

"*Sobinoff*! and *Neshdanova*? But she must have been –

"How did *you* come to hear of them?" He looked really amused and intrigued then.

"Why, I have records of them both."

"Not originals?"

"Oh, no. Re-pressings. But –"

And suddenly they were both talking rapidly about records and singers of the past. "Like two people in the opera queue," thought Mary, stunned. And with another

15

part of her consciousness she was delightedly aware that the haunted look had gone from his face, and he was animated and concerned only with what they were discussing.

They were still talking when the car slid smoothly to a standstill outside the entrance to the Gloria. He looked up then and said, a little uncertainly, "Oh – the Gloria –"

"Yes. Mr. Deane said to tell you that we got your usual suite for you. He said –"

"But I don't want the usual suite!" There was no mistaking the harsh certainty of that. And he looked at Mary as though she had suddenly become an enemy.

In a second she realised why. *Of course* he wanted nothing familiar. Nothing to remind him of those other times.

"You don't have to have the usual suite," she said calmly. "I'll go in and change the reservation now. Just see that Carter takes out all the baggage."

Carter would have been furious if he had known that anyone was casting such a slur on his efficiency. But Mary was doing no such thing, of course. She was merely giving Nicholas Brenner a reason for waiting outside while she slipped into the hotel and changed that hideously tactless reservation.

She accomplished it in a matter of minutes, and without fuss or explanation. By great good luck an equally suitable suite was available in a different part of the hotel. This was a matter of happy chance, as Mary well knew. But Nicholas Brenner when he came in seemed to think it was evidence of first-class efficiency on her part.

He thanked her, briefly but approvingly, and then said, "There's a rehearsal for principals this evening, I see. Will you be there?"

She opened her mouth to say that no such suggestion

16

had been made. But something far more than her immediate desire to go – some unerring instinct which was to inform many of her reactions in these first days of knowing Nicholas Brenner – made her reply that if he would like her to be there she would certainly come.

"I should like you to be there," he said without elaboration. "Pick me up here at five."

She promised to do so and went out to rejoin Carter.

"Is that the usual thing, Carter? Do we ferry them to and from rehearsals, and generally hold their hand?"

"Not with him we didn't in the old days. But that was when *she* was there," Carter explained. "She drove. And she gave the orders too, I might say."

"Oh," said Mary, who had not quite thought of Monica Brenner in that light. "Well, he wants me to go to rehearsals with him. Can we pick him up here at five?"

"Sure," Carter agreed. "Do you want to go back to the office now?"

Mary said she did. And back once more in her office she began to clear up the routine business of the day. Early in the afternoon her employer telephoned from Paris, and she was able to report that Nicholas Brenner had arrived, was safely installed at the Gloria, where he had decided to have a different suite from his usual one, and that he wanted her to go to rehearsal with him at five o'clock.

"Wants you to go to rehearsal with him?" echoed Dermot Deane's voice. "Whatever for?"

"I don't know," replied Mary with truth.

"Never happened with Miss Evans." She heard her employer laugh. "Oh, well, I suppose in Monica Brenner's day things were different. Fortunate that you had a free evening."

"Yes," said Mary, not thinking it necessary to mention that as soon as she had heard Nicholas Brenner required her company she had jettisoned a proposed theatre visit without question.

Half an hour later the switchboard girl rang to say there was a personal call for Mary and could she take it?

"Yes, of course." And she waited expectantly, half convinced that it must be Nicholas Brenner once more requiring her personal attention.

It was not his voice, however. It was a voice which, a year ago, would have sounded more wonderful to her than anything that ever wafted itself across the footlights. And it said,

"Mary! This is Barry. I've had the devil of a time tracing you. They didn't want to give me your new number at that cautious old solicitors' office. Since when have you changed jobs?"

"Hello, Barry." She cleared her throat and tried to make her voice sound light and casual. "I came to work for Dermot Deane, about three weeks ago. How – how come you're in London?"

"I've been transferred back to our head office."

"From Edinburgh? And how about – Elspeth?" There was a time when she would have thought she could scarcely pronounce that name, but it came out fairly trippingly when she made the effort.

It was he who left a moment's pause before he said, "That didn't work out, Mary."

"Didn't – work out? You mean you're not married, after all? Or do you mean –?"

"I mean she married another chap four months ago. Someone with rather more money than I have, and a great deal more of what it takes, I guess."

18

She really hardly thought that possible. For Barry, in her view, had more than his fair share of "what it takes". Oh, much, much more. That was why, when he became engaged to Elspeth Horton, life had lost all its savour and joy for a while.

She had pulled herself out of that slough of despond by now, of course. She was a year older, a year wiser. She knew that she had been a fool to suppose that anyone of Barry's particular make-up would fall for her type. He needed someone far more sophisticated, more worldly, more accomplished. Someone like Elspeth Horton.

And yet Elspeth had turned him down eventually, it seemed. For the first time in her whole relationship with him, compassion for Barry flooded over her, and her heart warmed afresh to him.

He was talking again now. "These things happen, Mary. They hit one between the eyes at first, of course. But it's no good being crushed and bitter about them."

Oh, she knew that! She knew that very well. That was the way she had talked to herself when he first became engaged to Elspeth and went away out of her life. But now he was back again. He was in London – and asking her to meet him again, that very evening.

Suddenly her mental processes shifted gear, and she exclaimed distressfully, "Oh, I can't, Barry. I'm terribly sorry. Not this evening. I – I have to go to rehearsal with one of our top clients."

"A rehearsal? What do 'our clients' do, then?" He sounded amused rather than impressed.

"I told you – I work for Dermot Deane, the impresario, you know. We – I mean he – handles most of the big musical stars. People like Oscar Warrender and Torelli and – and Nicholas Brenner."

19

"But surely people like that can get to a rehearsal on their own by now? Every little chorus girl in Shaftesbury Avenue can do *that*. Whose hand have you got to hold tonight?"

"I'm *not* holding his hand. It's Nicholas Brenner and —"

"The tenor?"

"Yes."

"Good heavens, Mary, you're not going to stand me up for a tenor? He's probably frightful when he's not singing. Wears patent leather pumps and a fur-collared coat, I expect."

"No," said Mary coldly, "he does not. At least, he didn't when I met him this morning. And anyway —"

"You only met him this morning, and he wants to take you out this evening? He's a fast worker, even for a tenor."

"He is not taking me out," Mary insisted patiently. "My boss is away in Paris —"

"I say, you do live it up in your new office, don't you?"

"So I have to deputise for him," concluded Mary, ignoring the interruption. "It's merely a question of giving polite and efficient treatment to an international star."

"Are you cross with me, darling?" asked Barry's voice coaxingly.

"No, of course not." She had been, but when he called her "darling" in that particular way she felt all the pain and bitterness of a year ago drain from her. "Barry, I'm truly sorry not to be able to come with you this evening. But ask me another evening. Please do! I'd love to see you and talk of old times and —"

"New," he supplied, in a tone which stirred the long-suppressed feeling of joyous excitement which she had always associated with him. "All right, make it tomorrow."

"Tomorrow would be perfect," she assured him, hoping anxiously that Nicholas Brenner would not require her then.

"Are you still living at home?" Barry wanted to know before he rang off.

"Yes, certainly."

"My good little home-bird!" He laughed, but tenderly rather than mockingly. Then he arranged where they should meet, and as she replaced the receiver Mary found that she was trembling slightly. Even now, and at the end of a telephone wire, Barry could still do that to her.

"But I've learned a lot since that terrible mistake a year ago," she assured herself. "I'll know not to take things too seriously this time. Just to enjoy the moment – play it lightly – not to assume too much just because he calls me darling and looks at me in that special way."

She telephoned her mother then, to explain that she would be late home. And then she added casually, "You'll never guess who phoned. Barry Courtland. He's back in London."

"Oh? – On a visit?" She knew her mother too well not to detect the faint reserve in her tone.

"No. He's come back here to work. He – Elspeth Horton didn't marry him after all, Mother. She married someone else some months ago." Then, as her mother said nothing – "He wanted me to go out with him this evening. But I couldn't, of course."

"That was a good thing."

"Oh, Mother! Why?"

"Because, dear, if I may say so, you were once far too ready to drop everything and do whatever he wanted. That's not good for any man, you know."

"No," agreed Mary thoughtfully. "Nowadays, I

21

wouldn't do that, of course. I'm older – and perhaps a bit wiser."

And only when she had rung off did she remember the theatre ticket in her handbag, which was not going to be used now because she had agreed to go to rehearsal with Nicholas Brenner instead.

He was waiting for her in the hotel vestibule when she arrived.

"I'm not late, am I ?" She glanced quickly at her watch.

"Not at all. And I hope I'm not interfering with your plans for the evening. I forgot to ask about that. Were you doing anything special ?"

"Not a thing," lied Mary cheerfully, mentally sinking the theatre performance – and even Barry – almost without trace.

"Then perhaps you'll have dinner with me afterwards," he said, as they drove eastward towards the rehearsal studios.

"Oh, but you don't have to bother about me like that." She smiled frankly at him. "I can quite easily –"

"It isn't a bother," he said gravely. "I should like your company, if you will have dinner with me."

She thought perhaps he was thinking that he would like any company rather than his own. And suddenly she was tremendously aware of the identity of that bright, golden girl who had been killed, and guessed that he could not bear to be alone on this first evening in London without her.

"Of course I'll come. It's terribly nice of you to ask me," she said.

Although Mary had occasionally been able to attend a public dress rehearsal in the Opera House, she had never before been to anything so intimate and close-range as a

22

rehearsal for principals. Oscar Warrender, who was to conduct the "Carmen" performances, was himself at the piano when they entered the studio. And his wife, Anthea, who was to sing Micaela, was also there.

Mary noticed that they both greeted Nicholas Brenner as a well-liked colleague. No reference was made to the tragedy which had happened since they last met, but Anthea Warrender's manner was warm and friendly to a degree, and even her famous husband relaxed something of his usually cool, remote air.

The Carmen, who came in a few minutes later, was a French Canadian. As famous for her acting as her singing, Suzanne Thomas was more emotional in her greeting to Brenner, whom she kissed on both cheeks.

"I'm so desperately sorry, darling," she said in a low husky voice which was perfectly natural to her although it sounded rather too good to be true. "You know how we all feel. I don't have to say anything, but —"

"No, Suzanne, you don't have to say anything," he agreed curtly. But he touched her cheek in a way that softened the abruptness of that.

Warrender then took over, cutting short further emotional exchanges, and Suzanne Thomas pushed back her sable jacket from her shoulders and dropped it into Mary's waiting hands, a little as though she expected a slave girl to be standing just there.

Anthea, on the contrary, smiled and said, "Oh, thank you, Miss Barlow," when Mary took her coat. "You are Miss Barlow, aren't you? Mr. Deane told me about you."

Mary was charmed. First that Dermot Deane should have spoken about her in any way that was in the remotest degree memorable, and secondly that one of her most admired sopranos should actually bother to recall her exact identity.

The other members of the cast came in then, and the rehearsal began.

Mary had wondered in her innocence why an intensive rehearsal was called for when each one of the principals was already internationally famous in his or her role. But when she saw and heard the imagination and intensity they put into their work, and the skill and artistry with which Warrender wove the well-known musical strands into a glorious, ever-fresh whole, she realised that this unremitting work was one of the good reasons why they *were* all world-famous.

She could not warm to Suzanne Thomas as a person, but as an artist she was riveting. And, although this was not essentially a rehearsal for acting, the way she used a flick of her hand or a glance from her long, dark, provocative eyes to convey sensuous appeal was a lesson in stagecraft.

Or perhaps it came quite naturally to her? Mary was not quite sure. Certainly she had never before seen any woman with quite so much animal magnetism.

It was, of course, the business of the tenor to seem enslaved and entranced. And this Brenner did to such good effect that Mary began to wonder if he and the Frenchwoman were half in love with each other. Then she remembered Monica Brenner and the recent tragedy, and reproached herself for being so naïve as to be taken in by what was simply superb acting.

Having settled that to her satisfaction, she could revel contentedly in the vocal feast spread out before her – the pure lyricism of Anthea Warrender's voice, the dark, sultry appeal of Suzanne Thomas, and the thrilling brilliance and power of Nicholas Brenner's tones.

She knew the expression "a voice of metal". But she had never before realised so exactly what this implied. Although Nicholas Brenner could run the full gamut from low-voiced appeal to heroic declamation, what gleamed through the texture of the voice again and again was the glint of pure gold. It was like shafts of light illuminating the darkening drama. And Mary, sitting there with her lips slightly parted in sheer wonder and delight, could scarcely believe that she was being privileged to hear all this at such close quarters.

They did not go straight through the work, but they ended with a good deal from the last act. And as Anthea was not required for this she came and sat beside Mary during the final heartbreaking scene.

"Nick almost *kills* one with that final appeal," she muttered to Mary. "No one else does it with quite that mixture of fury and despair."

"She's wonderful too," whispered Mary in all fairness.

"Oh, yes. No wonder he murders her," returned Anthea rather cryptically.

Then the rehearsal was over and they were all picking up their wraps and talking at once. And Mary overheard Oscar Warrender say to the tenor, "You're in remarkable voice, Brenner. It's got back that burnished quality you used to have three years ago."

"Thanks." Nicholas Brenner smiled briefly. Then he turned to Mary and said, "Ready?"

She was — on the instant. But before they could take their leave Suzanne Thomas put her hand lightly on Brenner's arm.

25

"Nick, you're not running away, are you? I was hoping we could have a bite to eat together and discuss —"

"Not tonight, my dear. You must excuse me. I flew over this morning and it's been a long day. Another time."

"Well, of course —" She allowed her glance to slide over Mary in a speculative, not very friendly way. Then she seemed to decide that this inconsiderate young person was there for no purpose but to pick up wraps, carry scores, check timetables and generally make herself useful.

"*A bientot,*" she said with a satisfied little nod, and turned away. Brenner and Mary went out to the waiting car.

"Where to, sir?" enquired Carter.

"Somewhere quiet, where the food is good, the wines better, and no one will ask me for my autograph," replied Brenner comprehensively. "Where does Mr. Deane go when he wants a bit of privacy?"

"Leave it to me, sir," Carter said. "Shall I drop you anywhere, Miss Barlow?"

"Miss Barlow is coming with me," the tenor stated without emphasis but in a tone of cool decision. And if Carter found anything unusual in the arrangement he made no sign of doing so.

Within twenty minutes he deposited them at the inconspicuous entrance of a small, exclusive restaurant which answered in every particular Nicholas Brenner's stated requirements. He was then dismissed with a courteous good-night and the information that he would not be required any more that evening.

Feeling shy but elated, Mary preceded her famous escort into the restaurant, where they were immediately installed at a secluded corner table. She tactfully saw to

26

it that he was seated with his back to the room, so that in the unlikely contingency of anyone coming in who might recognise him, he would not attract undesired attenion.

Over the choice of the meal he consulted her meticulously, but over the wines hardly at all, for which she was glad since her knowledge of wines was sketchy in the extreme. When this was done, he sat back with an air of genuine relaxation and asked, as though it really interested him to know her opinion, "How did you enjoy the rehearsal?"

"Beyond description!" Mary told him truthfully. "I never heard great singers at such close quarters before. I'm still a bit dazed by the experience."

"Did we make such a noise, then?" he enquired amusedly. "It can be quite shattering in a smallish studio if you're not used to it, I know."

"Oh, I didn't mean *that*!" She was a good deal shocked. "It was, of course, much louder than anything I'm used to. But what was so terrific was — I suppose one would have to call it the emotional impact. I've heard 'Carmen' more times than I could say, but this was like being personally involved in the final tragedy."

"That's how it should be." She thought he was pleased by her choice of words. "To tell the truth, I seldom even rehearse it myself without that sense of tremendous involvement. I think it's the same with any reasonably sensitive artist."

"I overheard Mr. Warrender say your voice was in specially good form," she volunteered presently. "And I don't think I ever heard you sound more wonderful."

"No? It's partly the long rest, of course."

"And partly —?" she invited him to finish that.

But his expression went curiously bleak and he said,

"Partly something quite else – I think. But never mind about that now."

"I'm sorry," she said quickly, feeling that perhaps she had sounded inquisitive rather than pleasantly interested.

"You have no need to be." His slight smile absolved her of any such suspicion and made her feel disproportionately happy. And then, between courses, he said unexpectedly, "Tell me something about yourself."

"About *me*? There's really nothing much to tell," Mary protested. But because there is no sweeter flattery than to have those words uttered by someone who interests one, she proceeded to give him a brief, but not unamusing, account of her family background and her working life.

"And in your out-of-office hours?" he wanted to know.

"I'm primarily an opera and concert fan, as I told you. I used to think when I was much younger –" she missed the smile which that drew because she was intent on her story – "that perhaps I might be a singer myself. But I found I really hadn't anything like enough talent. So I enjoy myself as mere audience."

"But you don't go to these performances all on your own, surely?"

"Oh, no! There are quite a crowd of us. Friends, acquaintances, even a few enemies when it comes to fighting about rival favourites," she conceded with a laugh.

"But no one special person?" he persued, apparently with genuine curiosity.

"You mean – am I engaged or anything?"

"I suppose I did. But perhaps that's inexcusably inquisitive?"

"No." Mary shook her head. "I don't mind your asking." Again she had realised that he was asking about her

28

life because he had no wish to sit there reflecting on his own. "I don't imagine it's a very interesting story for anyone famous like you. You must know all sorts of fascinating people and —"

"Tell me, all the same."

She laughed a little shyly and turned her wine-glass on its stem. And suddenly she found that she truly did not mind his asking about her. In an odd way, it was even something of a relief to talk to someone about Barry. Someone so far removed from her own private life that he was as safe a confidant as anyone.

"It must happen to a lot of girls, I'm sure," she said reflectively. "I was very much in — I was keen on a man who quite suddenly got engaged to another girl. It's about a year ago, and I've got over it now, in a way. Enough to realise that I was very silly even to suppose I was his type or —"

"What was his type?" Nicholas Brenner wanted to know.

"Oh, something much more sophisticated and worldly than I am. More — more *interesting*, you know."

"No," he said, "I don't think I do know. What is so interesting about being sophisticated and worldly?"

"Well —" began Mary. And then, as she seemed to find that difficult to define, he said,

"Never mind. Go on. Did he marry the other girl?"

"No, he didn't. That's the odd thing —"

"Not odd at all," Nicholas Brenner assured her lightly. "Quite a number of men wake up just in time."

"You're really very good for my sagging morale." She laughed outright at that. "But I didn't mean his not marrying her was odd. I meant —" she hesitated. Then she shrugged and completed the story. "The odd part of the story is that I found out only today. He's come back to live in London, and he rang me up this afternoon, in the office."

"Just to tell you he was not married after all?"

"No, not only that. He wanted me to go out with him this evening."

"But, my dear, you should have gone!" Nicholas Brenner looked genuinely put out.

"I had a prior engagement," she reminded him with a rather mischievous smile. "I was going to rehearsal with you."

"But I would have understood! — At least, I think I would," he added with a touch of rather engaging realism about himself.

"It wasn't necessary," Mary assured him. "On the contrary, it wasn't a bad thing to be able to say 'no'. I used to say 'yes' all too often in the old days, I think."

"Ah, well, that's another thing!" He laughed with genuine amusement. "But —" suddenly something about her seemed to arrest his attention completely — "I see you have recalled something which is worrying you. You look dismayed all at once. Are you thinking it would have been better —"

"No, it's not that." Mary looked past him with widened eyes. "It's just that — someone I know has come into the restaurant."

Nicholas Brenner was not a highly perceptive artist for nothing. His curiously light hazel eyes regarded her with a touch of half cynical understanding.

"I suppose, by one of those coincidences that only happen in real life, the young man in question has just come in?" he said.

"Y-yes. How did you know?"

"By your expression. And also – life's like that. It often plays that kind of malicious trick." He spoke with an unaccountable bitterness which could have nothing to do with her and her inconsiderable affairs, she felt.

"Has he seen you?"

"Not yet – no. He's talking to another man who came in with him."

"Then change places with me if his presence embarrasses you."

"But you'll be facing the room then, and you wanted to avoid notice."

"The young man is hardly likely to ask for my autograph, even if he happens to recognise me," retorted Nicholas Brenner with a touch of humour. And, as unobtrusively as possible, they changed places so that Mary now had her back to the room.

"All this must seem rather small and silly to you," she said apologetically. But he disclaimed this immediately.

"If you want to know, I'm rather enjoying myself," he declared. "If the young man comes this way do you want me to play the part of a rival admirer?"

"No, of course not! In fact I feel I should apologise for having involved you at all in my unimportant affairs."

"Please don't. It's a refreshing change. You forget I've just come from rehearsing a scene of frantic jealousy and despair. I don't at all mind reversing the situation and inflicting the same thing on someone else."

She laughed at that and felt the sense of tension relax.

"I don't think Barry is likely to feel jealousy or despair over anything I do," she said frankly.

"Shame on him," replied her companion. "He must be a very insensitive – or unappreciative – young man."

And then he allowed her to drink her coffee in silence

31

while she reflected on the pleasing implication of his words. Presently she asked him one or two questions about the role he had just been rehearsing, and from that they passed to the other part he was to play during the season.

"Mr. Deane described Lensky as 'not a killer role'," she told him with a smile.

"Well, it isn't, of course, in the sense of length or sheer expenditure of energy," he agreed. "But it calls for something like faultless singing, and it contains in my view one of the loveliest and most testing of all tenor solos. In addition —" he smiled suddenly with a sort of mischievous frankness which surprised her — "I rather fancy myself in the high hat and caped coat of the period. If one has to be shot in a duel one should at least be allowed to look romantically interesting beforehand."

She laughed out loud at that, and he said softly, "Your admirer is looking this way. Ye-es, I think he's recognised that nice fresh laugh of yours. He's getting up and coming over."

"Oh —" she was so unprepared for this that she looked put out, and he lightly put a reassuring hand over hers as it lay on the table.

The next moment Barry stood before her, his eyes alight with pleasure, interest and frank curiosity.

"Hello! What are you doing here?" he wanted to know.

"I'm having dinner with Mr. Brenner," she explained a little unnecessarily. "The rehearsal is just over." Then she quickly made the introductions and the men exchanged polite if not specially cordial greetings.

"I'm afraid I forestalled you and had already claimed Miss Barlow for this evening," the tenor said carelessly.

"For a rehearsal — yes. She told me about that," Barry agreed, with a certain smiling exactness which was something less than friendly. "But tomorrow it's my turn, I believe."

"I'm not sure. We hadn't discussed tomorrow," replied Brenner pleasantly.

"But Mary and I have, and the arrangement is made," Barry returned, just as pleasantly.

"In that case —" Brenner made a regretful little gesture towards Mary, who was rather enjoying this in a frightened sort of way.

"Yes, tomorrow — as we arranged," she said quickly. And before she quite realised what she was doing she had given Barry a cool little nod of dismissal which would have been unthinkable in the old days.

He withdrew, in reasonably good order, and Brenner said, "Shall we go now?"

"Yes, of course." With a touch of anxiety she remembered his telling Suzanne Thomas that he had had a long and tiring day. "I expect you want to get back to your hotel and to bed."

"Oh, no!" His slight grimace of distaste disclaimed any such idea. "I'll take you home first."

"But you can't do that! I live out in the suburbs. And anyway, it's quite an easy journey by bus. I do it twice a day."

He said no more about that, but called for the bill. Then he put on her coat for her with an air of rather more special attention than was called for, she thought, and followed her through the restaurant. As they came abreast of Barry and his companion he gave them a faintly lordly bow which is peculiar to most stage celebrities when

33

they wish to make their weight felt. It was so different from his almost unobtrusive entrance an hour and a half ago that, when they were outside on the pavement, she could not help asking, "Why did you do that?"

"Why did I do what?"

"Bow in that over-gracious way."

"Oh —" he laughed. "That's what's called 'putting on the tenor'," he told her coolly. "I thought the young man deserved it."

"Because of the way he treated you?" she asked diffidently.

"No. Because of the way he treated *you*," was the unexpected reply. Then he raised his hand to summon a cruising taxi and asked, "Where to?"

"The Gloria, I suppose."

"No, I'm taking you home." He spoke as though the subject had not been previously mentioned. And because further protest would have been ungraceful she gave him her Hampstead address and got into the taxi with him.

As they drove north she left the silence unbroken for a few minutes. Then she said with feeling, "Mr. Brenner, I don't know how to thank you. This evening has been a sort of opera-lover's dream. To go to a private rehearsal and then to be taken out to dinner by the star of the occasion —"

"One of them," he murmured modestly.

"The brightest one," she retorted with pleasing partiality. "And then that you should show such kind interest in the affairs of an unimportant member of the audience —"

"No member of the audience is unimportant to a public performer, Miss Barlow," he said amusedly.

"Oh, in a sense, I daresay. But you gave me most of

your evening. It was wonderful of you."

"Didn't you realise that I was *glad* to occupy myself with someone else's affairs on this particular evening?" he said suddenly, and all the laughter was gone from his face and his voice. "It's I who should be thanking you for this evening. You can have no idea how I loathed and dreaded the thought of this first evening in London."

He spoke with such bitter intensity that for a moment she was struck dumb. Then she said gently, "I think I do understand. At least, so far as an outsider can understand someone else's tragedy. It was the idea of being alone, wasn't it, in a city where you and your wife had been so often together?"

He nodded slightly.

"That applies to several other cities, of course." He spoke more calmly now. "It was the thought of the first few days in any one of them that made the idea of a come-back so insupportable. I think – perhaps – I shall never mind quite so much again."

Mary was so truly moved that it was a moment before she could say anything.

"I'm glad if I helped in any degree," she said simply at last. "I know it's no good saying, 'Try not to think of this – or that.' Particularly with anyone so absolutely memor-able as your wife. I saw her more than once at the stage door. She was so radiant and perfectly beautiful, wasn't she?"

"Yes, I think she was the most beautiful woman I ever saw."

"I'm so terribly sorry." Quite without thinking she put her hand warmly over his. "Did you love her very much?"

His hand turned slowly and held hers in a grip that hurt.

35

"No," he said, with almost frightening deliberation. "In the end I hated her. That's why I find it so hard to live with myself now. I was driving the car when it happened, you see. In a way, I killed her."

CHAPTER II

MARY caught her breath on a slight gasp. Then she rallied all her common sense and said deliberately, "You're exaggerating, you know. You didn't kill her. You're so emotionally involved that you're recalling everything in the wrong terms and tormenting yourself quite unnecessarily."

"You don't know anything about it!" he retorted angrily.

"Not about the exact circumstances, that's true. But do you suppose this sort of reaction doesn't come to most well-intentioned people? Almost everyone who has lost someone in a tragedy thinks afterwards, 'Oh, *why* did I say or do – or even think – this or that?' It's quite natural. Don't get things out of proportion."

"They were out of proportion already," he said moodily. "There had been times when I almost wished her dead. And then, suddenly – she was."

His marvellously flexible voice dropped quite naturally to a near-whisper, and the compelling theatricality of the scene was such that Mary had to make a real effort not to yield over much to its spell.

"Did you have any real reason for wishing her – for feeling like that, I mean?"

"I thought so. But —" He stopped and gave a short, incredulous little laugh. "You strange girl! You don't sound even remotely shocked."

"Oh, I am — inside," Mary admitted. "But that's not important. If it makes you feel better to talk about it —"

"In some odd way, it does." He spoke half to himself.

"Then we'd better stop the taxi and get out here," she said practically. "We can walk across this corner of the Heath. If we go on driving we shall be at my home in five minutes."

So they got out, he paid the driver and they struck out across the Heath, at first in silence. Then, as though for a moment she impinged on his consciousness as a person, instead of just a sounding-board for his spoken thoughts, he said, "You're not cold, are you?"

"Not at all. But it's I who should be asking you that. You're the one who has to be in good voice for Don José next week," she reminded him. At which he laughed and drew her arm through his and said thoughtfully,

"José — who killed the woman he loved."

"Am I supposed to draw some interesting parallel from that?" she asked rather crisply, determined not to let him indulge in too many histrionics, however naturally they might come to him.

"Not really." He looked faintly abashed, and then said rather engagingly, "You think I'm a bit of a show-off, don't you?"

"No more than a famous tenor is entitled to be," she assured him a little indulgently. "But I suppose you're trying to tell me that you *were* in love with — with your wife to begin with?"

"But of course! She — well, you've seen her for yourself — one could hardly help falling in love with her. And

38

when things began to go wrong it wasn't only her fault, of course. I'm not specially easy to live with. Few successful theatre people are, I suppose. We tend to live too much with our nerves at full stretch."

"We'll allow you that." Mary smiled slightly. "So you were difficult and she – I suppose she was so lovely that other men ran after her, which made you jealous?"

"Not at first. Oddly enough, it was she who became jealous first. You see – it sounds idiotic, I know – but there's something about a voice, particularly a tenor voice, which does things to –"

"Oh, you needn't tell *me*!" Mary's gay laugh eased the tension. "From stalls to gallery there's hardly one woman who remains unaffected by a tenor of quality. He can look like a pig and still do considerable execution. And if he looks like you – well, it's really quite unfair."

"I don't really understand it" – he sounded genuinely mystified as well as amused. "But it certainly makes for problems at times. The difficulty was that she loved everything connected with the fame and success and – glamour, if you like – which are part of a successful singer's life. She couldn't have enough of that, so long as I wasn't singled out for any personal attention. That did make her jealous. And so she began to – compete, I suppose is the word. To show that she too could attract people if she liked. – I'm not really explaining this very well, because it's still a sort of horrible puzzle to me. I don't know myself at which point we lost touch."

"One seldom does, I expect," Mary said sadly.

"I just suddenly woke up to the fact that my wife was deliberately playing off other men against me. After that the rows started. Bitter, scarifying rows in private, but with a pleasant, smiling façade kept up in public. I got so that I didn't know if I acted more on the stage or off. Then that last morning –"

He stopped as though someone had put a hand round his throat. But she said quietly, "Go on."

"As usual, we quarrelled about something utterly trivial – a question of who should drive the car. I insisted. I drove it. There was an accident. And she was killed."

As though by common consent, they came to a halt, and Mary turned to face him.

"Was the accident your fault?" she asked steadily.

"I don't know." He put his hands on her upper arms and gripped them hard, without apparently realising what he was doing. "I don't know. And I never shall. That's what takes the joy out of everything. Even singing."

She was so overwhelmed by the scene that she very nearly fell then and there into his arms in a welter of shared sorrow and sympathy. But fortunately, just in time, her practical streak asserted itself with some force. And, somewhat to her horror, she heard herself say,

"There's no need to be melodramatic about it. And stop playing the melancholy Slav! Why shouldn't you know, for goodness' sake? To begin with, was any other car involved?"

She could almost feel the salutary shock run through him. Then he said, rather like a subdued schoolboy answering up at a difficult examination, "I ran into a parked lorry. It was on the wrong side of the road and –"

"Then it was *not* your fault!"

"If I'd been more alert, more on the lookout for what was ahead. But she'd just said something wildly provocative. I turned my head to throw a violent reply at her – and the thing happened."

40

"Then still less was it your fault," Mary stated firmly. "I'm terribly sorry for her, but the fact is that she even provoked the inattention which caused the accident. For you to talk about having killed her is just self-dramatisation."

There was an extraordinary silence, and Mary suddenly recollected that this was a very famous artist whom she was almost bullying about his most private affairs. She was so shocked that she actually shut her eyes for a second and waited for the lightning to strike. Instead of which, to her immeasurable surprise, Nicholas Brenner leant forward and kissed her quite deliberately.

"As a melancholy Slav," he said, with unmistakable laughter in his voice, "I can only say 'thank you' for that chastening deluge of British common sense. What is your other name, by the way? I can't go on calling you Miss Barlow after all this."

"It's Mary," she said in a very small voice. "And I don't know what came over me. I'm terribly —"

"Mary —" He savoured it with some amusement. "Yes, of course, it would be. Well, Mary, I don't promise *never* to play the melancholy Slav again, but —"

"Oh, please! May I take that back?"

"No, you may not. It's all too accurate. We do rather like dramatising ourselves, you know, and being interestingly sad. I'm sure your brand of common sense is good for one."

"You're being very kind," Mary said remorsefully. "And please don't think I'm unsympathetic, or that I'm not very, very grateful to you for a most wonderful evening. — I have to turn off here. This is my road, and that's my home over there. The small house with the white door."

41

He looked across with interest and asked, "Do you live there on your own?"

"Oh, no, with my parents. I told you about them over dinner, but perhaps I didn't explain that I live with them."

Momentarily, she had a crazy impulse to invite him in to meet them. But, although her father and mother were inclined to take things very much as they came, she felt that perhaps a famous tenor at this hour of the night might tax even their equanimity.

So instead she directed him to the nearest taxi rank and was just about to leave him when he said, "Will you come out with me again, Mary?"

She hesitated a moment, divided between the longing to accept immediately and the uneasy feeling she should remind him who she was.

"If you find you have time for – for Mr. Deane's secretary –"

"Tomorrow evening?" he suggested, apparently oblivious of the hint.

"I can't tomorrow, I'm afraid," she reminded him. "I'm going out with Barry."

"The unappreciative young man who wanted to marry someone else? Very well, another time." Then as she turned away he caught her lightly by the arm and drew her back again. "Are you going to tell him that I kissed you?" he asked with unmistakable amusement in his voice that time.

"No, of course not. It was just a momentary – Well, a sort of impulse that was half a joke."

"So *that's* what you thought of it!" He was amused still, but she realised that he was slightly nettled too. "Well, dismiss it that way if you like. But this is deliberate." And he tipped up her chin and kissed her firmly on her lips. "How about that?"

"A splendid stage exit," she retorted, and managed to produce a very casual little laugh in her turn. Then she pulled herself away and ran up the path to her home without looking back.

But once she was inside the house she leant against the door, the back of her hand against her lips.

"I'm quite mad!" she thought. "Quite, quite mad. That was Nicholas Brenner who kissed me – deliberately. And I *adored* it!"

"Is that you, Mary?" her mother called out at that moment from the back room.

"Yes, Mother." She went in immediately.

"I thought I heard you come in. What a long rehearsal it must have been! Aren't you starving, you poor child?"

"Oh, no. No, it's all right, Mother. I went – I was taken out to dinner afterwards."

"By Barry?" Mrs. Barlow was shrewd enough to make that casual rather than curious.

"Barry?" Mary had no idea how completely her tone dismissed Barry. "No. By Nicholas Brenner."

"Dear me!" Her mother put down her knitting at that and regarded her child with interest. "On your own, do you mean?" And then, as Mary nodded, she picked up her knitting again and said, "That must have been quite exciting, going out with a famous singer. Or is he rather dull off stage? These people sometimes are, I believe."

"No, he wasn't a bit dull," Mary stated judicially. And then, as that seemed faint praise indeed for the most exciting person she had ever met, she tried again. "He was

43

extremely kind, and looked after me charmingly. He wouldn't let me come home alone. He brought me all the way by taxi. Wasn't that nice of him?"

"Extremely," her mother agreed. "Very proper behaviour."

Mary thought about that last kiss and felt that "proper" was perhaps not quite the right word in that particular context. So, instead of enlarging on that she launched into a lively account of her day, knowing how her mother enjoyed hearing about her doings, even though she never displayed unwelcome curiosity. And, to her surprise, she found that she could talk about Barry without any self-consciousness, even adding to her account the fact that he had not been specially pleased when he came into the restaurant and found her dining with Nicholas Brenner.

"I think I like the sound of Nicholas Brenner," said her mother inconsequentially. At which Mary laughed and kissed her good night and went off to bed feeling inexplicably lighthearted.

The next morning Dermot Deane – who had flown back from Paris the previous evening – was in the office almost as early as Mary. And in answer to her sympathetic enquiries about his trip, he admitted cautiously that all had gone exceedingly well.

"One never knows with Torelli, of course. She always plays hard to get, on principle. But once you've got her she's more reliable than all the younger ones put together. She's probably shortened my life by at least ten years, over the time I've known and dealt with her, but I adore the woman. How did the rehearsal go?"

"Marvellously! At least, *I* thought they were all perfectly marvellous, and Mr. Warrender seemed pleased.

44

And then Mr. Brenner took me out to dinner."

"On your own?" enquired Dermot Deane, as her mother had done, but in a rather different tone.

"Yes. Was it all right for me to go?"

"If you thought so – most certainly." Her employer laughed. Then he leant back in his chair and regarded her with amused interest and said, "You're quite a dark little horse in your way, aren't you?"

"No!" Mary was rather indignant. "Why do you say that?"

"Because I was wondering just how you snitched him away from under the very nose of Suzanne Thomas. Didn't *she* want to go out with him?"

"Yes," admitted Mary reluctantly, at which Dermot Deane laughed immoderately.

"But he was tired – and he'd already asked me," she explained earnestly. "Besides, he was depressed about – about being in London for the first time alone since the accident. Suzanne Thomas is a bit high-powered if one's feeling depressed, don't you think?"

"*I*, my dear? If you're asking me personally, Suzanne Thomas is a great deal too high-powered for my taste, however I'm feeling. So he parried her advances, did he, and took you out instead? I said you were a dark horse."

And after that they got on with the day's work.

All day Mary was too busy to spend any time musing on the previous evening, but she was vaguely, though illogically, disappointed to arrive at the end of the afternoon without hearing anything of or from Nicholas Brenner. Not that she was expecting him to contact her personally, of course. But she felt somehow that *something* about him or his activities should have required her willing attention in the office.

45

Instead, she had to spend a great deal of time over the affair of a very boring German baritone who had an exaggerated idea of the value of his lieder recitals in the international music scene.

So long did he detain her while he explained himself, in great detail and two languages, that she knew she was going to be at least a quarter of an hour late for her appointment with Barry. And she had just flung the last file into the filing cabinet and was about to reach for her coat when the phone rang again.

Great was the temptation to ignore the wretched thing. But her official conscience stabbed her too fiercely, so she seized up the receiver and rapped out the number with something less than her usual courteous tone.

There was a second's pause. Then Nicholas Brenner's voice asked doubtfully if that were Miss Barlow.

"Mr. Brenner!" She was not aware that the change in her tone was very nearly comical.

"It didn't sound like you," he said.

"I'm so sorry, I didn't realise it was you. I thought you were a boring baritone who –"

"Please! Insult could hardly go further. To be mistaken for a baritone is in itself a shock to any self-respecting tenor. But a *boring* baritone –"

She found herself laughing more than she would have thought possible after her irritating afternoon.

"I take it all back! What can I do for this anything-but-boring tenor?"

"Nothing, if you still insist on going out with the undeserving Barry whose surname I have forgotten."

"The name is Courtland. And I do insist on going out with him this evening. I promised," Mary stated firmly.

"I see. Well, have a moderately good time. But not such

46

a good time that you feel he is entitled to a lot of your attention in the near future. Will you come with me to the Warrender concert on Friday evening?"

"Oh, I'd love to!" cried Mary impulsively. "But have you got tickets? It's a sold-out house, you know."

"There is no such thing as a sold-out house," he told her carelessly. "Dine with me first, will you?"

She bit back the eager acceptance which sprang to her lips.

"Mr. Brenner, don't think this is inverted snobbery or anything. But I am just the girl in the office, you know. It's terribly kind of you to invite me to the concert and I'll be delighted to come. But the other might be a bit – a bit too much. You know what I mean, I'm sure."

"No, I'm afraid I don't," said his voice courteously at the other end. "Do explain."

"Oh –" she glanced at the clock, suddenly remembered the waiting Barry and exclaimed, "I can't explain over the phone. Please may I just accept for the concert, without the dinner?"

"No," he said.

"Did you say –?"

"I said 'no'. I'm being temperamental. All tenors are allowed to be temperamental. It's one of the perks of the job."

She began to laugh again, spontaneously and irresistibly. She had never before known anyone who could make her laugh in quite that way. But she remained firm.

"I'll love to come to the concert with you, but I'm afraid I just can't dine with you first. Shall I meet you near the box office at the Festival Hall about a quarter to eight?"

There was quite an astonished pause. Then he said, "If you say so – yes."

47

"Thank you very much. And now I simply must go."

"Yes, I expect Barry is waiting," he agreed, with a certain note of satisfaction in his voice.

In spite of all her efforts, and some luck with a taxi, Mary was very late indeed when she breathlessly joined Barry and began to make her eager apologies.

"It doesn't matter." He kissed her as though he had every right to do so – which perhaps he had, she supposed, if one thought about the past. "How very pretty you're looking, Mary! Where did you get all that sparkle and vivacity?"

"It's because I've been hurrying," she said quickly.

"It certainly is not!" He laughed and drew her arm close against him. "It's something much more subtle than that. Something or someone has kissed the sleeping princess awake."

"I don't know what you mean!" She was genuinely startled, because his laughing words recalled all too vividly the way Nicholas Brenner had kissed her.

"You needn't take that too literally!" He laughed, but he glanced at her as though something about her stirred his amused interest quite powerfully. "It's just that you've grown up – stopped being a home-bird and flown out into the world to make it your own. Something like that. It doesn't matter what, but it's very attractive, my sweet. Has anyone told you that you've grown into a beauty over the last year?"

"No. But my employer told me today that I was a dark horse," she replied, and laughed in her turn. "Not quite such an engaging description, I'm afraid."

"But even more intriguing – and full of interesting possibilities. Oh, Mary, how good it is to be with you again!"

It was good to be with him too. However much she

might tell herself that she would be more careful this time and take nothing for granted, nor let her feelings run away with her, the fact was that it was wonderful to be laughing and talking with Barry once more.

She had missed him horribly. Only now could she bear to think how horribly. Over the long months she had made herself accept the fact that he was no longer any affair of hers. He belonged to another girl. Acceptance of that fact had hurt desperately, but somehow she *had* accepted it. And now here he was, back again with no strings attached.

No longer need she put those agonising restrictions on her heart and her hopes. At least, only those restrictions which added wisdom might dictate. She was free to let her cramped feelings expand again. Cautiously perhaps, but without any sensation of guilt. And if his eager, laughing, admiring glances meant anything, he was suddenly finding her far more attractive than he ever had before. Charming and pleasing she once might have been. But now she was intriguing and captivating.

"Has he changed? or have I?" Mary asked herself, as she lay in bed late that night thinking over her evening with Barry.

She would have been less than human if she had not been elated and uplifted by the discovery that she was suddenly important in his eyes. Not only her heart, but her pride too had taken a terrible bruising over his defection to Elspeth Horton. It was only natural to feel good now when she realised that something about her puzzled and charmed Barry in a way he obviously found infinitely attractive.

"You're learning rapidly," observed Dermot Deane to her during the following morning. And although, naturally, *he* was referring to her grasp of the work, deep down inside Mary was the warming conviction that she was learning rapidly in other ways too.

Aloud she said, with sincerity, "Everything about the work in this office is so interesting. One *wants* to learn."

"Well, I suppose that's true." Her employer grinned reflectively. "There are times when I ask myself why I stay in the maddening game. But I'm a star-gazer by nature, even now. And I know I'd just wilt — so far as someone of my build can wilt — without the alarms and crises and triumphs and sheer thrills of the game. Can you make time to go along and see Suzanne Thomas this afternoon, by the way?"

"Why, yes, of course, if you want me to." Mary did experience the faintest qualm at the thought of Suzanne Thomas, though why she was not quite sure. "She's staying in a rented apartment off Hill Street, isn't she?"

"Yes." Dermot Deane picked up a parcel. "She would like to have this new score of Dickenson Price. I shouldn't have thought it would be up her street, but she wants to look it over and asked that you should take it along."

"Me? — personally?" Mary looked surprised. "I should have thought—"

"That any junior on the staff could have done the job," Dermot Deane finished for her. "So should I. But those were Her Ladyship's words: 'Could your Miss Barlow bring it along?'"

"I didn't know she even knew my name," said Mary.

"Nor I. But don't ask me what's in her mind. I never make wild guesses with my clients. If you don't want to go—"

"I don't mind at all," Mary insisted a little disingenuously. The exact truth was that her curiosity was stronger

50

than her vague feeling that she did not like, nor wish to know more of, the attractive French Canadian.

These mixed feelings were still with her when she entered the block of luxury flats that afternoon and was wafted upwards in a silent lift to the sixth floor where Suzanne Thomas had her London home.

She opened the door herself, bestowed on Mary a lazy but more friendly smile than any she had displayed so far, and said,

"Do come in. It was nice of you to bring the score along. I know it was tiresome of me to be in such a hurry to see it. But when I get excited about a work I just have to know right away if it's for me or not."

"I can understand that." Mary did her best to match the friendly smile with one of her own, while she concealed her astonishment at being pressed to stay and have tea, with such charming insistence that there was no graceful way of refusing.

"Have you been long with Dermot?" Suzanne Thomas asked as she poured the tea. "He's a marvellous person, isn't he?"

Mary was able to agree with this sentiment quite sincerely, adding that he was a very good employer and that even three weeks in his office had been long enough for her to discover that.

"You've been there only three weeks? I suppose you worked for one of the other agents before that?" She spoke with such apparent friendly interest that it was hard (though not impossible) to think that one was in some way being cross-examined.

"Oh, no." Mary explained how she had taken the chance of transferring from the legal world to the music world largely because of being an enthusiastic listener.

"So it was just from the audience that you get to know Nick Brenner so well? Did you know her too? — Monica."

The questions followed so rapidly and yet naturally upon each other that Mary found herself replying, just as naturally.

"But, Miss Thomas, I don't know Mr. Brenner particularly well, and I never knew Mrs. Brenner at all."

"No?" The famous mezzo gave a sceptical little smile. "Yet he seemed to regard you almost as a family friend the other evening. He wouldn't go out with me —" she laughed that off, apparently without rancour — "but he was perfectly ready to go with you."

It was, of course, quite ridiculous to be called on to explain the situation as though it *required* explanation. But Mary realised that to refuse to satisfy this woman's curiosity would give the incident an entirely false air of importance. So, briefly but a little coolly, she explained about having been assigned by her employer to look after Nicholas Brenner on the day of his arrival.

"As I was quite new to the job I just said 'yes' to everything Mr. Brenner suggested," she said with a smiling shrug.

"And he suggested your going out with him after the rehearsal. You must have made quite a hit, Miss Barlow."

"No." Mary kept her temper with difficulty. "I think his first evening back in London was full of unhappy memories. And the fact that I was quite unconnected with the past and, to tell the truth, quite unimportant made it less of a strain to be with me than with anyone more intimately connected with his affairs."

"Well, I suppose you could be right." Suzanne Thomas's smile was almost completely frank and friendly that

52

time. Almost, but not quite. And after a moment she said, "It was very sad about Monica, of course. But I expect you know that she had become such a problem that, in a dreadful way, her death was a sort of solution to a very unhappy situation."

"Miss Thomas, apart from casual queue gossip, I've known absolutely nothing about the private lives of these rather remote people, until I came to work for Mr. Deane. And from neither source have I heard anything of what you are implying," Mary stated firmly.

"Didn't Nick say anything, when he took you out?"

It was an impertinent question in all the circumstances, and Mary had no qualm of conscience about lying outright.

"Of course not! He doesn't strike me as the kind of man who would gossip about his personal affairs to the girl in the office. Which is really all I am, you know, when all's said and done."

"You underestimate yourself." But Suzanne Thomas laughed with genuine amusement. And for the first time Mary felt that she was at last satisfied. Indeed, she made no attempt to detain Mary further and, taking the Dickenson Price score, she tossed it carelessly on to a pile of music with such palpable indifference that Mary almost winced for the hapless composer.

By the time she got back to the office she was feeling sufficiently annoyed about the trumped up visit to say frankly to her employer, "It was just an excuse to get me along there and pump me."

"About what? Your going out with Brenner?"

"Yes. How did you guess?"

"There's nothing this wise old owl can't guess, given a

few salient facts," retorted Dermot Deane with some satisfaction. "She was always after him. She was Monica Brenner's best friend. And if there's a bigger menace than a best friend in this business, I've yet to meet it. Now Monica's gone, Suzanne will probably go all out for him herself. And she doesn't mean to be pipped at the post — by you or anyone else."

Mary laughed angrily.

"Even she can't be so idiotic as to imagine *my* pipping her at that particular post," she said tartly. "I've only met the man twice. Once, as you know, I had the routine job of fetching him from the airport, and once I had to accompany him to a rehearsal with half a dozen other people."

"But you went on to dinner afterwards, my dear. There's the rub." Dermot Deane laughed. "On to dinner afterwards."

"Only because I was quiet and undemanding company," she countered quickly.

"Maybe." Dermot Deane rubbed his chin meditatively. "Quiet and undemanding company. That must have been a novelty. Well, well, the test will be if he repeats the invitation."

To her furious embarrassment, Mary immediately felt her colour rise, the more so as her employer continued to look at her with amused attention.

"I said you were a dark horse. Why are you blushing?"

"I'm not blushing! But you make me feel self-conscious when you say such silly things. Anyway — I may as well be frank about it — Mr. Brenner told me he happened to have two tickets for the Warrender concert tomorrow and he asked if I would like one."

"And you happened to say you would, I take it?"

54

"Do you know anyone who would have *refused* a ticket for the Warrender concert?" Mary countered with spirit.

"No," said Dermot Deane, "I don't. Enjoy yourself. But — and now I'm not just teasing you — watch your step if Suzanne Thomas is around."

Mary said soberly that she would. But this talk of the Warrender concert had suddenly brought it into clear and exciting focus. Something not just to be dreamed about, but to be actually experienced. She even spared a few regrets for the fact that she had rejected the dinner invitation which had originally gone with it. Though after the silly episode with Suzanne Thomas she knew more than ever that she must tread warily.

"Not that I want to put a stupidly exaggerated importance on to what was probably the most casual invitation," she assured herself. "If it had been anyone else who asked me —"

But it had not been anyone else. It had been Nicholas Brenner. And Mary was beginning to see that one could not make even the simplest arrangement with a very famous artist without having to consider all sorts of cross-currents which simply did not arise in the case of a pleasantly undistinguished friend.

This fact was brought forcibly home to her as she waited for him the following evening near the box office at the Festival Hall. Afraid of being late and keeping the great man waiting, she of course arrived much too early. So that inevitably friends and cronies of her gallery days came up from time to time to exchange a word or two, ask how she was getting on in Dermot Deane's office, and give her their candid opinion of various artists they had all been hearing during the last week or two.

It was the usual pleasant give and take of gossip and

views, and ordinarily Mary would have thoroughly enjoyed it. Now, the thought that Nicholas Brenner might appear at any minute and cast a blinding ray of reflected glory round her made her feel nervous and self-conscious.

Finally someone asked carelessly where she was sitting that evening. And, feeling like a parvenu apologising for her Rolls-Royce, she said vaguely, "I think – in the stalls."

One of her friends whistled. But another one said, "I suppose you got a complimentary, being in Dermot Deane's office? – Or, there's Nicholas Brenner. He looks a bit older since the accident, doesn't he? but terribly distinguished. He's looking round for someone."

"He's looking round for me," said Mary, in an unnecessarily small voice. And at the concerted gasp which greeted this statement, she felt somehow as though she were showing off. That was what made her say hastily, "No, please don't rush off. I'll introduce you."

Stunned, as only star-gazers can be stunned when starlight turns full upon them, her friends stood rooted to the spot, and Mary found herself saying, a little nervously, "Mr. Brenner, may I present one or two of your most devoted admirers? We're all looking forward immensely to the 'Carmen' next Wednesday."

Immediately and effortlessly, he turned on them what Mary was to come to know later as "the full tenor treatment". Nothing could have been more charming than the way he accepted the introductions, lingered for a moment or two to talk, and then courteously ushered Mary in the direction of their seats, while the dazzled fans made their happy way to the upper reaches of the hall.

"Thank you for being so nice," Mary said in a rather

subdued way, as they took their seats in the hall.

"To your friends? But, my dear girl, why shouldn't I be? Quite apart from their being your friends, they're my public. And no artist should underestimate his public. Without them, we don't exist, you know."

"That's true in a way, I know. But I wasn't really showing you off," she explained in a confidential burst of frankness.

"Weren't you. I rather hoped you were?" He flashed a quick, laughing glance at her which did odd things to her.

"Well, I felt terribly proud of being with you, of course," she admitted with engaging naïveté. "But also I didn't want them to think I was brushing them off in any way just because my job in Mr. Deane's office gave me a chance of coming here with a celebrity."

"Dear, you do worry about the oddest things." Nicholas Brenner laughed softly. "Firstly, no one who knew you would expect you to be disloyal to your friends. And secondly, if you were, I shouldn't like you as I do. Does that satisfy you?"

"Yes," murmured Mary. And she stared down fixedly at her programme so that he should not see any telltale radiance in her face.

"He called me 'dear' and said he liked me! — Oh, perhaps that's just part of his way of being charming to everyone. — But I don't think it is. — And I must manage to look up and be sensible. — But I can't. If I pretend to look at my programme a little longer —"

And then she realised that he had risen to his feet and was greeting someone who was coming slowly up the gangway. She did look up then. And immediately the warmth of her delight was quenched in an indefinable chill.

He was speaking to Suzanne Thomas, superb in black velvet and sables. And though her faintly sensual mouth was smiling, she was looking past him at Mary with eyes that were as hard and cold as flint.

CHAPTER III

AFTERWARDS, Mary thought one of Oscar Warrender's finest achievements of the evening was that he almost made her forget Suzanne Thomas was sitting just across the gangway. Almost – but not quite.

As the glorious strands of music which made up her favourite Beethoven symphony wound themselves round her heart and senses, Mary did feel that little else mattered. But, somewhere at the back of her mind, was the nagging wish that Suzanne Thomas were sitting in any other part of the hall. Without leaning forward Mary could not actually see her. But, as though there were a sort of emanation of dislike and hostility from the famous mezzo, she was painfully aware of her presence without needing to see her.

In the interval Nicholas Brenner asked if she would like to come out for coffee or a drink. But Mary, feeling rather like a snail which sensed safety only in its shell, shook her head.

"No, thank you. I'd rather sit here and do my homework –" she smilingly indicated the programme notes. "The Bruckner is quite unfamiliar to me. But you go. Lots of people probably want to talk to you."

He made a slight grimace at that, but he went. And, as he got up, Mary saw to her relief that the seat across the gangway was empty. The last thing she wanted was an exchange of doubtful courtesies with Suzanne Thomas, and she thankfully bent her head over her programme and concentrated on the rather involved notes.

For some minutes the voices of people round her were no more than a general hum and murmur. Then her quick ear detected the familiar, attractively husky tones of Suzanne and it took her only a second longer to identify also the clear, pretty voice of Anthea Warrender, the conductor's wife.

She was saying, "But of course we're expecting you after the concert, Suzanne. It's a supper party for friends and colleagues. I glimpsed Nick Brenner in the hall, but lost him again. I hope he'll come too."

"I doubt it." Mary knew instinctively that the mezzo was making her utterance specially clear. "That rather pushing girl in Dermot Deane's office has managed to get hold of him. She won't let him go if she can help it. She's sticking like a leech at the moment and he doesn't quite know how to get away."

"Really?" Anthea sounded surprised and a little put out, Mary thought, as she lowered her head still further so that she should not be identified. "I thought she seemed rather nice and retiring —"

"Oh, my *dear*!" Suzanne's laugh spoke volumes.

"One could ask her too, I suppose." Anthea sounded faintly obstinate.

"Truly, I wouldn't do that." The other woman sounded very much in earnest suddenly. "She's something of a menace in her quiet way. And for Nick's sake she shouldn't be encouraged. She's quite equal to going after Oscar too, I shouldn't wonder."

Anthea laughed quite gaily at that and said she would

60

back Oscar to look after himself. But that if Suzanne thought an invitation would create problems for Nick, it might be better just to leave him out – though it was a pity.

Then the voices faded away, as the two singers moved off to speak to someone else, and Mary was left sitting there with rage and humiliation in her heart, and a very high colour in her cheeks.

As though she would have *dreamed* of pushing her way into a party of distinguished artists! And at the same time, as though she would want to do Nicholas Brenner out of the pleasure of joining his friends after the concert. She wished passionately now that she had never let him involve her – and himself – in anything which could cause such embarrassing complications.

She could tell him, of course, that she had to go straight home after the concert – which was, indeed, what she had intended to do. But, recalling his insistence on taking her home the other evening, she doubted if he would accept this. Especially if he heard about the supper party and had some idea that he might be slighting her.

"Oh, dear!" thought Mary, "there's such a thing as being almost *too* polite and scrupulous about the formalities." Though not often in this age, she was bound to admit.

If only – And at that moment Barry Courtland dropped into the vacant seat beside her and said, "Hello! What are you doing here, all on your own?"

"Barry!" She had never been more pleased to greet him. Not even when he had turned up with the news that he was not married to Elspeth Horton after all. "Are *you* here on your own, too?"

"I am." He smiled at her a little quizzically.

"Are you doing anything afterwards?"

"Not unless you're coming with me for a coffee and a sandwich somewhere."

"Oh, I am! I am," Mary assured him with almost hysterical relief. "Look here, I'm not stampeding you into entertaining me or anything. But here comes Nicholas Brenner — you're sitting in his seat, by the way, and had better get up — and when I tell him you're taking me home, please back me up."

"But of course!" Barry was obviously both surprised and intrigued. "Is he making himself a nuisance?"

"Oh, no!" That was all Mary had time for, because Nicholas Brenner joined them just then, nodded in a distantly courteous way to Barry and quite obviously waited for him to go.

"Thank you, Barry. Then I'll meet you at the bottom of the main staircase afterwards," Mary said, with a dismissing sort of glance. And, as Barry made off, back to his own seat, Brenner said drily,

"What did that mean, exactly? You're coming round backstage with me afterwards and then out to supper."

"Oh, I'm not — really." She managed to make that surprised but emphatic. "*You'll* be going round backstage, of course, and I overheard Anthea Warrender saying there was a supper party and that you were expected —"

"And why shouldn't you be expected too, if you're my companion for the evening? Unless we chose to go out on our own, of course."

"It never entered my head." Mary managed to look all surprised innocence. "I mean — it's marvellous of you to have let me have one of your tickets, and I'm enjoying the concert more than I can say. But I wouldn't even want to go to that sort of party. I'd be quite out of my element.

And certainly the Warrenders wouldn't expect me there. I doubt of Mr. Warrender even knows who I am."

"There are such things as introductions." She was astounded and dismayed at the unmistakable shade of anger that came over his expressive face. "You introduced me to your friends. Why shouldn't I introduce you to mine?"

"But it's *different*," whispered Mary beseechingly, as the leader of the orchestra entered to the sound of applause. "Please don't be angry. I thought I – I was arranging everything for the best."

"Then you were mistaken," he replied coldly. And he turned from her and directed the whole of his attention on Warrender, who was now making his way past the first violins to the conductor's desk.

She tried to say something else. But not only had the conductor now picked up his baton. Nicholas Brenner seemed in some strange way completely and utterly removed from her. It was not just that he would not look at her. After all, one hardly expected to exchange significant glances during a serious concert. But there was a sense of absolute withdrawal, something intangible but so final that she felt sick and chilled with dismay.

Through the silent hall there came the first delicate opening phrases, but Mary was entirely oblivious of them. Never in her life had she felt more miserable and rebuffed. She didn't care about Bruckner or anyone else. She only wanted to be friends with Nicholas Brenner again.

She turned her head slightly and tried to will him to glance at her. But he looked steadfastly ahead, grave and unsmiling. She told herself angrily that he was just "playing the melancholy Slav" again. But there was nothing in that phrase now that would make them laugh together.

She doubted if they would ever laugh about *anything* together again. Their friendship had been a precious but fragile thing. And now, with her stupid self-consciousness about doing the right thing in unfamiliar circumstances, she had spoiled everything.

Presently she accepted the rebuff of his absolute indifference and stared down at her programme, trying to control the slight trembling of her hands.

The moment she noted that they *were* trembling she felt an increased nervous tension. She could not stop that absurd quiver. She could only watch, fascinated, while it grew slightly more pronounced. And at the same time she was aware of a tightening of her throat muscles and a stinging in her eyes.

"Stop it!" she admonished herself silently. "You can control yourself if you have to. It's no worse than trying to stop a cough in a pianissimo passage!"

But it proved just as difficult. And only by continuing to keep her head bent could she give any semblance of composure. That was why, as she stared down at her unsteady hands, she saw immediately when his strong, well-shaped hand came over hers and held it still.

She was so grateful, so relieved at this sign of renewed friendliness, that she would have liked to look up and smile. She blinked her lashes, to clear any absurd moisture from her eyes. And as she did so, one large, ridiculous, unmistakable tear fell on the back of his hand.

There was no possibility of his being unaware of it. His grip tightened for a moment. And, under cover of a useful passage from the French horns, he said softly, "I'm sorry."

"I'm sorry too," she whispered.

And, incredible though it seemed, she and Nicholas

Brenner continued to sit there more or less hand-in-hand for the first movement of the Bruckner. And Bruckner's first movements can be pretty long.

In the few moments of pause between the first and second movements he released her hand and, while people stirred, coughed or murmured a word or two to each other, he said quietly, "You can go out with Barry, of course, if you want to. I didn't mean to upset you."

"And I didn't mean to be interfering," she told him. "Only I thought you would certainly want to go out with your friends, and I didn't want to complicate things by –"

"Ssh!" said someone behind, rather officiously, considering that the music had not yet started again. But Mary accepted the hint and tried no more explanations. She just sat there thinking how wonderful and upsetting and bewildering the evening had been, and how, in a strange way, it would be something of a relief just to go out with the blessedly ordinary Barry afterwards.

It did not strike her as epoch-making that Barry, of all people, should seem blessedly ordinary in contrast to some of her recent experiences. *Barry!* who had once been the disturbing centre of her existence.

At the end of the concert, when at last the waves of applause had subsided, Nicholas Brenner held Mary's coat for her and said, "You don't even want to come round backstage?"

"Not tonight, if you don't mind. This is a good moment for us to separate. It's natural for you to go round there – with Anthea Warrender and – and Miss Thomas and the others. I'll slip off and join Barry. We go the same way home anyway. But I can't thank you enough for having brought me here. It's been a wonderful evening."

"In spite of –?"

"Are you coming backstage, Nick?" enquired Suzanne Thomas's voice rather imperiously at that moment. And he bade Mary good night and went off in the wake of the black velvet and sables.

Hardly knowing if she were disappointed or relieved, Mary made her way to the bottom of the main staircase, where Barry was waiting to take her off to a favourite coffee bar. It was obvious that his curiosity was greatly tickled and that he felt entitled to ask some questions by now.

"Why did you need to give Brenner the brush-off?" he wanted to know. "Had he been getting fresh or something?"

"Not at all!" she was rather indignant. "But there was a supper party for some of the stars afterwards — Oscar Warrender and his wife were giving it — and I didn't want Mr. Brenner to think I expected him to drag me along to it too."

"But he wouldn't have thought that, surely, just because you happened to be sitting beside him?" Barry seemed to think she was making rather heavy weather of the incident. And she was not at all sure that he wasn't right.

"Actually he had got the ticket for me," she explained airily. "They were almost impossible to get, you know. And so I was in the awkward position of being with him and yet not with him, if you know what I mean. The last thing I wanted was for him to feel reluctantly compelled to look after me when the concert was over. Your turning up like that was absolutely providential."

Barry said he was only too glad to be the instrument of Providence in this particular case. Then he teased her a bit about what he called her conquest, and warned her

66

that tenors often liked to fancy themselves as lady-killers.

"I'm safe enough," Mary declared with a laugh. "I don't know that I shall even see him again. Except from the gallery on Wednesday. Are you coming to the first-night 'Carmen'?"

"No. The second one."

"I might be there then too," Mary said carelessly, having no intention whatever of missing any of them. "From what I saw and heard at rehearsal, I should think Suzanne Thomas is a terrific Carmen."

"Was she the rather sultry-looking piece in black velvet and sables?" Barry wanted to know. And Mary said she certainly was, and managed to laugh instead of wincing as she recalled the unfair and humiliating things Suzanne had said of her.

In spite of telling Barry that she hardly expected to see Nicholas Brenner again before the first night – and then only from afar – this was not quite how Mary really expected events to work out. But they did. She heard nothing. Not so much as a phone call. And as she was kept busy at the office on the day of the dress rehearsal she had no opportunity of attending that either.

Her employer "looked in for Act Two" as he put it and reported favourably.

"Brenner is in great form. I never remember hearing him better. It's as though –" he stopped and then added with apparent irrelevance, "Sad about Monica, of course. But she had him on a pretty tight rein during that last year. I suppose there's a sort of relief in being footloose again. Are you going to the first night?"

Mary said she was. That she had a good seat in what is now rather snobbishly called "the rear amphi", but which still remains the gallery to all true devotees.

67

"Well, I suppose it's often more fun up there than downstairs," Dermot Deane remarked indulgently. "What it is to be young and limber!"

Mary laughed and agreed. And on the night of the performance she was happy indeed to be back in her familiar haunts, in company with friends with whom she had shared so many operatic thrills in the past. Outwardly she was just the same girl, enjoying vicariously the emotions which a great performance can provide. But inwardly she had never before been so deeply and personally involved. The anguish of Don José was the anguish of Nicholas Brenner; and to a degree she would never have believed possible, Mary found herself sharing this with him.

In real life she liked Suzanne Thomas little enough, but she admitted freely to herself that here was the finest Carmen she was ever likely to see or hear. And as she watched these two great artists moving inevitably towards the destruction of each other, it seemed to her that she was witnessing something more than a stage performance.

At the end there was that rarest of all tributes – a deathly hush, succeeded by storms of applause.

"On, it was wonderful! – wonderful!" declared Mary's neighbour, in absolute ecstasy. "What a pair! How gorgeous they look together."

Mary regarded them through her opera glasses, and thought reluctantly that they did look gorgeous together.

"Is he mad about her in real life too?" Mary's neighbour wanted to know. "He looks it."

"How should I know?" asked Mary crossly.

"Well, Jennifer said you know him. Don't you?"

"A little – yes," Mary conceded. "But he hasn't got round to telling me about his love-life yet."

Her neighbour laughed appreciatively, and then returned to the willing exertion of clapping her hands until they hurt. On and on the applause went, and it was a long time before they reluctantly rose from their seats and straggled down the stairs into Floral Street, still arguing and enthusing about the performance.

Here they split up – still reluctantly – into those who had to hurry off for trains or buses and those who could linger for the final indulgence of standing round the stage-door for a last glimpse of their favourites, when they emerged in their real identity.

To this last group Mary attached herself, though she stayed somewhat in the background, not quite sure if she hoped to be noticed or overlooked. It was quite a long, cold wait. Then the Warrenders came out together, in company with the rather dashing baritone. Smiles and a few autographs were dispensed, though Warrender cut the business rather short and hustled his wife out of the cold into a waiting car. Then there was a concerted murmur of "Here she comes!" and the heroine of the evening stood in the doorway, with the tall figure of Nicholas Brenner behind her.

Somehow, Mary had not expected that they would come together, and she drew back hastily into the shadows, certainly not wishing to be noticed now. Meanwhile, Suzanne – radiant, lovely and triumphant – borrowed a pen from Brenner and stood there scribbling her name on programmes for the eager autograph-hunters.

He watched her with an indulgent smile, Mary noticed from her place at the back of the crowd, and something about that gave her a slight but disagreeable shock.

Then suddenly Suzanne cried good-humouredly, "Enough, enough!" and she made for her car, which was parked on the other side of the street. Brenner paused a minute longer to satisfy two final requests. Then he turned to follow her and in that moment the crowd parted unexpectedly, in the way crowds do when the principal attraction is on the move, and he came face to face with Mary.

"Why, hello!" he stopped immediately. "Where were you tonight?"

"Up in the gallery, cheering for you. And Miss Thomas too, of course," Mary added as an afterthought.

"Then why didn't you come round afterwards?"

"I – I didn't think I was expected," Mary said.

"Well, you were." But he smiled full at her, this time without a trace of reproof for her having guessed wrong about what she should do. "Are you coming to any of the other performances?"

"Yes, of course. All of them."

He laughed at that, rather delightedly.

"Then come round on Friday. – Coming, coming," he called to Suzanne, who had sent a long, musical, "Ni-ick –" from the car. And he actually touched Mary's cheek lightly before he left her and went off across Floral Street.

"What did he want?" One of Mary's friends came up to her and ran a mockingly awed hand down her coat-sleeve. "I'm just seeing if a bit of the stardust will rub off on me."

"He said I could go round to his dressing-room on Friday," Mary said, still a little dazed. And then she had to run for her train, and as she ran she wondered if Suzanne had noticed with whom he had exchanged those few words at the stage-door, and, still more, if she had noticed the gesture which accompanied those words.

No Thursday had ever been so long as the one which divided the Wednesday of the first "Carmen" from the

Friday of the second one. Mary was afraid of every tiny mishap which might conceivably come between her and the promised visit backstage. And Barry's rating (though fortunately he was unaware of this) dropped almost to the level of a nuisance when she thought how it might be difficult to detach herself from him after the performance and go round to Nicholas Brenner's dressing-room on her own.

In spite of all her fears, however, everything worked out quite simply in the end. Barry was sitting downstairs that evening. She saw him, from her rather lofty perch, as he strolled out in the interval in company with an extremely well-dressed blonde. There had been a time when this sight would have brought a sobering chill to her spirits. But tonight she merely reflected thankfully that he was unlikely to be looking round for herself after the performance.

Once more the masterpiece and its splendid exponents worked the familiar magic. Once more the expert hand of Oscar Warrender guided the performance to a triumphant conclusion. And when it was all over Mary made her way down to the street and along to the stage door, feeling very faintly sick with mingled excitement and nervousness.

At the stage door she hesitated instinctively, for there is a wide, though subtle, gap between those who stand *around* the stage door and those who GO IN. Until then Mary's place had been unmistakably outside. Now she felt something of a gate-crasher as she finally pushed her way past the crowd and presented herself before the searching glance of the stage-doorkeeper.

"May I go up and see Mr. Brenner, please?" she said as boldly as she could. "He is expecting me."

Perhaps she only imagined the faint pause, or perhaps her inner sense of insecurity made her think she had not made good her case. At any rate, with what she felt was brilliant inspiration, she added firmly, "I'm from Mr. Dermot Deane."

"That's all right." The doorkeeper waved her on immediately. "Do you know the way? Turn right and then left and up the stairs. Mr. Brenner's in Room Two."

Mary followed the directions, pausing for only a moment to give a nervous glance at her reflection in the big mirror outside the chorus room as she passed. Then, with her breath coming a little unevenly, she mounted the stone steps to the next floor.

In the narrow corridor at the top there were already several people waiting, some of them outside Room Two and some outside a room from which Mary easily identified the sound of Suzanne Thomas's voice raised in gay excitement. She stood irresolutely by the wall, trying not to look as out of her element as she felt, and watched while the favoured ones went in and out. Each time the door of Room Two opened she tried to decide whether or not this were the right moment to enter. But each time her courage failed her, and she pressed her back against the wall again, seeking some sort of support.

It looked as though she were going to be the very last one. But then who was she to push in before these other confident, elegant, self-assured people? As the last group came out of Nicholas Brenner's room she moved forward with a little spurt of confidence. But his dresser looked out and said briskly, "You'll have to wait a few minutes. He's changing now."

Feeling almost as though she had made an improper advance, Mary retreated to the wall again, sorely tempted now to slip off without making any further attempt to see him. But to have come so far and then not to have even a word with him was not to be endured. She would just wait until he came out and then —

And at that moment, Suzanne came out of her room accompanied by two or three people in evening dress. She allowed her glance to travel over Mary with the blankness of deliberate non-recognition. Then she rapped smartly on Brenner's door, put her head round and called out clearly, "Good night, Nick."

"Good night," he called out in return.

Suzanne withdrew her head, glanced at Mary again and then, still in that clear tone and speaking through the half-open door, she added, "Here's your most persistent fan hanging about outside. Haven't you got a word to say to her, you hard-hearted man?"

The gay mockery of her tone made almost a joke of these shaming words, and her companions laughed in indulgent chorus as they glanced passingly at Mary. Stripped of every vestige of dignity or significance, Mary felt the colour rush into her cheeks and then away again with a force that almost turned her dizzy.

Then Nicholas Brenner's voice said, *"Who?"* and he pulled open the door and stood there shrugging on his coat.

Perhaps it was because he too, in his time, had been subtly humiliated by a few laughing words that he took in the scene and its implications instantaneously. He knew that rescue must be total or not at all.

"Why, darling!" His handsome, rather tired, expressive face suddenly registered the utmost pleasure. "I wondered where you'd got to. I shan't be a moment. I'm almost ready." And putting out his hand he drew her against

73

him and kissed her in front of them all. "Good night, Suzanne," he said again with apparent good-humour, as he smiled over Mary's head at the famous mezzo, and he drew Mary into the dressing-room and pushed the door half closed.

Mary heard Suzanne say, "We-ell –" before she and her friends went off, laughing and talking. Then Nicholas's dresser asked, "Is there anything else, sir?" as he lifted down the last-act costume from its hanger.

"Nothing, thank you. We're just going." Brenner gave him a smiling nod of dismissal. And suddenly Mary was alone with him in the small dressing-room.

"Why did you do that?" she said at last.

He didn't go through the pretence of asking what she meant.

"It was the only form of rescue operation I could think of," he told her lightly.

"How did you know I needed rescuing?"

"I heard what Suzanne said – and the way she said it. I've been humiliated by a few words often enough in my time. Monica was good at it too. I'm sorry if I overdid it on the spur of the moment. Don't think too badly of me." He turned to the dressing-table to gather up a few personal things.

"I don't think badly of you," Mary said slowly. "I think you're the kindest and most understanding person I've ever known."

"You do?" He turned back to her and laughed. But it was a laugh which had an unexpected note of tenderness in it. "Well, I'm not sure you aren't the kindest and most understanding person *I've* ever known. At least you helped me in those first days here, in a way I could never over-estimate. Now we're going out to eat somewhere.

74

I'm ravenous — I always am after a performance. And please don't give me any of that stuff about being the girl in the office who can't go out with the famous tenor."

"I wasn't going to," said Mary submissively. And she went down the stairs with him and out at the stage door, not quite able to believe that this was really happening to her.

Afterwards she was quite unable to recall what she ate and drank with him that evening. What she most recalled was the way his exhaustion seemed to drop from him, and how life and vitality began to glow in him again like a light coming up in a recharged lamp.

Fascinated, she watched and listened as — gay and almost boyish in his enthusiasm, and totally unlike the rather melancholy creature who had talked to her that first evening — he spoke about the performance, explaining to her how certain effects were obtained and why the slight loosening of the tension in one place could make the final build-up almost unbearable.

"How you love it all!" She smiled at him almost indulgently. "I've never seen you like this before."

"That's because you've never been with me after a fine performance," he told her. "Beforehand I'm as nervous as a cat. Most of us are, I suppose. Nervous, irritable, unreasonable — knowing that one is and yet being quite unable to do anything about it."

"But once you're on stage —?"

"Oh, the moment I'm on stage I'm quite cool. At least, if someone like Warrender is at the conductor's desk. The coolness is only mental, of course. It's part of one's professional discipline. But it leaves one free to react completely to the drama both emotionally and artistically."

"It sounds alarmingly complicated!"

"No, it's glorious," he replied simply. "And then at the end, you're aware that you've achieved an artistic whole – something that the composer meant and heard when he put down those little black notes on the paper. If you can get that feeling it's wonderful."

"Did you get that feeling tonight?"

"Yes. Largely owing to Warrender. And Suzanne too, of course. She's a marvellous colleague when it comes to striking the divine spark." He laughed reminiscently, and she saw frank admiration in his face.

"Do you usually feel like that?" she asked him presently, partly perhaps to detach his thoughts from Suzanne.

"I haven't – for some time. That's partly why it was so exciting tonight." He hesitated, and then he added, "I don't want to rake up what is past and – forgiven, if you like. But that radiant bubble of achievement is so fragile. Criticism – or mockery – in those first few minutes can shatter it, and nothing can put it together again. One's nerves are raw, I suppose, just after a performance, and one is rather vulnerable."

"It's over," she said softly, seeing the sudden tension in the line of his jaw.

"Yes, it's over," he agreed, on a long breath. And the tension relaxed.

"Would it embarrass you if I told you you were so wonderful tonight that I cried?" she said slowly.

"No, darling. Few things embarrass me." He laughed as though he had not a care in the world. "Did you really cry?"

Mary nodded.

"I expect it was very naïve and unsophisticated of me," she admitted, "but –"

76

"That's what makes you lovable," he said. And while she was reeling under the directness and simplicity of that, he went on, "Most worthwhile artists have a deep strain of naïveté themselves. We continually find ourselves the centre of the scene, with lots of glitter and glamour. But do you suppose we don't cherish — and long for — the moments of simplicity? Basic things like laughter — and tears — mean far more to us than columns in any newspaper, or the pontification of so-called musicologists."

"Well, I can understand that," she laughed softly.

"Go on talking to me," he commanded, and he leant his forehead on his hand in a completely unselfconscious pose. "When you say things in that quiet, beautifully pitched voice of yours I feel all my nerves unwind contentedly and — Did anyone ever tell you that you have a lovely speaking voice?"

"No." She shook her head. "But I'm glad if you say I have."

"That first morning I met you —" he was still not looking at her and spoke as though half to himself — "you made me laugh. Do you remember? I felt I hadn't laughed naturally for ages, and you made me laugh quite spontaneously when you said you were a fan who milled round the stage door but didn't scream. Do you never scream, Mary?"

"Why should I scream?" Mary asked reasonably, but she smiled.

"Oh, most women do. With excitement or laughter or — anger. You can't imagine how that jars on a sensitive ear. But what were you saying?"

"Nothing. You were doing all the talking, and I was enjoying listening. But I'll talk if you like. Did you know that I very nearly didn't stay to speak to you this evening?

I felt shy, watching all those important people go into your dressing room. And then when I finally plucked up courage, it was too late. Your dresser said you were changing. It made me feel awful and very much an intruder. I expect that was why I was looking a bit dashed and forlorn when Suzanne — when Miss Thomas and her party came by. That's why she — said what she did. But I wasn't really *hanging about*, you know."

"I know, dear, I know." He looked up then and smiled. "You were just there because I very much wanted you to be there at that moment."

"Well —" she felt she should reduce that to something less significant, "you had said I was to come round, so I came."

"Are you coming to the first night of 'Eugene Onegin', to hear me sing Lensky?" he asked abruptly.

"Yes, of course. I have my ticket in the rear amphi."

"I want you downstairs," he replied imperiously. "I'll send you a ticket downstairs. I want you where I can see you."

"*See* me? But you can't see anything from the stage, can you?"

"The first row or two in certain lights. And when one comes before the curtain after each act."

"But why do you want to be able to see me?"

"Why do you think?" He laughed and looked straight at her in a way that made her heart skip an uneasy beat or two. "Because you're very good to look at, for one thing. For the rest — we'll leave that for another occasion. It's time I took you home now."

"Please — you truly don't have to take me home. Just put me in a taxi. You can even pay the fare in advance if you like," she added as he made a gesture of dissent. "But

78

please don't drag out to Hampstead at this time of night and after a strenuous performance. You — you worry me, when you insist on these things."

"Do I?" He looked amused. "How nice to have you worry about me. You almost tempt me to insist. I don't think I know of anyone else who worries about me, except to wonder if I'll turn up all right on the night of performance. May I really not take you home?"

"No." She touched his hand gently, so as to soften the briefness of that. But it was a firm negative all the same.

"Very well." He called for the bill and then they went out of the restaurant together.

It was a clear, cool night, and to Mary at any rate there was a touch of magic in the air. Even the taxi, which drew up at a sign from Nicholas, had a sort of aura about it. And when she heard her companion ask to be dropped at the Gloria before she herself was taken on to Hampstead, she realised that there were to be just a few more wonderful minutes before she had to part from him.

In the dark intimacy of the shared taxi he made no attempt to put his arm round her — rather to her disappointment, she was ashamed to realise! He merely said rather teasingly, "Well, have you been broken in now to the idea of sometimes coming out to dinner or supper with me?"

Mary hesitated, and he went on impatiently, "All right, I know you can't spend our time for ever talking to each other across restaurant tables. I'll think of something else."

She wanted to ask him what else he was likely to think of. But they reached the Gloria before she had got up quite enough resolution to do so.

He kissed her good night. And although she knew that stage people kissed each other very easily and on all sorts

79

of occasions, it gave her the strangest sensation to realise that for the first time she had kissed him back again. Then he got out and she saw him talking to the taxi-driver, who seemed very pleased about something.

"Are you free next weekend?" Nicholas came back and spoke to her through the open window of the taxi. "Not tomorrow. I mean next weekend."

"Why – why, yes, I think so." She was too startled to say anything but the truth.

"All right, I'll arrange something." Then he stood back and waved the taxi on, while Mary leant back against the worn leather of the seat-back and wondered just what he had meant by that.

She was not, it seemed, the only one who wondered. For as the taxi drew up outside her home and she got out, the driver – a stout, middle-aged man – leant towards her and said impressively,

"It's no business of mine, but I've got daughters of my own. Don't you go spending no weekends with that chap. He's a high-flyer and good-looking. But he gave me a five-pound note."

"Gave you a five-pound note!" Mary was scandalised. "Whatever for?"

"Ah, that's what *I* wondered. Just you be careful." And the driver flipped up his flag and drove off into the night, leaving Mary to gaze after him in mingled amusement and consternation.

CHAPTER IV

DURING the weekend Mary went over and over that evening with Nicholas Brenner in her mind. At one time, of course, the dazzling thing about it would have been the sheer thrill of being taken to supper by one of one's favourite opera stars. But now, in some way it was difficult to define, the heart-warming significance of it all was that it was *Nicholas* who had taken her. No other star would have supplied the same effect.

Everything else seemed ordinary in comparison. She loved her home and her parents. She had many other interests outside her passion for music. But, almost to her shame, she found the weekend stale and flat since it contained no contact with Nicholas.

On Sunday afternoon Barry telephoned, to ask if she would come out with him that evening. But instinctively she made some excuse about another appointment, and then was ashamed again when her mother, who had overheard the conversation, said in surprise, "Are you really going out this evening, Mary?"

"No." She shook her head. "I – just didn't want to go. I'd like a quiet evening at home. But he wouldn't have understood that, so I had to tell a white lie."

In Mrs. Barlow's experience Mary seldom told white

lies, and certainly it had not been her practice to put off Barry, of all people, with something less than the truth. She regarded her daughter thoughtfully.

"You haven't quarrelled with Barry, have you?"

"Oh, no, Mother! I'm just not quite so eager to go out with him these days. I don't really know why."

"Possibly because he treated you rather shabbily over Elspeth Horton," suggested her mother drily.

But Mary knew it was not that. She felt no rancour about Elspeth and Barry nowadays. In fact, she felt little emotion of any kind about Barry except for a good-humoured friendliness. With a slight sense of shock she accepted that discovery and all that it implied.

To her mother she simply said lightly, "I expect I've grown a bit wiser and more selective. Barry's good company and a pleasant friend. but that's all."

"I'm glad to hear it." Her mother gave a satisfied little nod. "And if by being more selective you mean you can now recognise the good, solid, down-to-earth qualities which make up the best type of man, that's all to the good."

Mary smiled non-committally, and immediately wondered if one could describe Nicholas Brenner as having the good, solid, down-to-earth qualities. She thought not, on the whole. He was highly-strung, superbly gifted, unpredictable, kind and yet arrogant in an engaging way – she got no further, because it occurred to her that almost everything about him was engaging. At least to her.

As the great star he had attracted her from afar. Now that she knew him at closer quarters he had become intensely human as well. The combination was almost irresistible. She could hardly imagine life without him now.

And at that discovery she experienced another shock — a much more powerful one this time. For of course she was going to *have* to imagine life without him. Indeed, to live most of her life without him. This was just a fascinating, slightly unreal interlude while he happened to be in England. In something like a month he would be gone — hundreds, perhaps thousands, of miles away. If she were lucky he might come to London again in a year's time, but perhaps not even then.

The thought was crushing. Almost literally so, for it brought with it a sharp anguish which made her gasp.

"It's no good being silly about him," she told herself. "He belongs to an entirely different world, probably an entirely different way of thought. What did he mean, for instance, about arranging something for next weekend?"

There had been no doubt about what the taxi-driver thought he meant! And perhaps to a man like Nicholas a casual shared weekend was no more than the natural next step in a growing friendship.

"But I'm not a weekend girl!" thought Mary. "He has no right to think of me like that." Or had he?

If that were to be her one gift from the gods so far as Nicholas were concerned, just how would she react? She was staggered and a good deal shocked to find that she had got as far as this even in her own thoughts. The whole line of argument was entirely alien to her usual pattern of life. But then *he* was alien to her usual pattern of life. Gloriously, bewilderingly, lovably alien.

She sat on the side of her bed that night with her head in her hands.

"I can't really be in love with him! What's the matter with me? I must be crazy to be thinking like this. Or am I just the kind of fool who falls for any man who makes a fuss of me? First Barry, and now – him."

But she knew this was not the case. There had been plenty of friends and admirers from time to time. But the only one who had really gained her affections had been Barry. It had been a disastrous experience in the end, but at the time her hopes and thoughts had followed a perfectly understandable line. She had believed Barry loved her. She had hoped he meant to marry her. All the greater had been the shock when he announced that he was going to marry someone else.

With Nicholas it was quite different. One didn't, if one were an inconspicuous secretary, expect to marry a world-famous tenor. One had a friendship – possibly a flirtation. In certain circumstances, if one were a different kind of girl, one presumably had an affair.

But that, Mary knew – or was pretty sure she knew – was not for her. Therefore she must be careful not to become too deeply involved. No weekend nonsense for her. But then, if that were the case, the sooner she drew back the better. Unless she wanted to be badly hurt again.

Monday dragged past without any word from Nicholas. She had to make a tremendous effort to keep her attention focussed on her work. If she were to become romantically scatterbrained about this or that operatic star she was not going to stay the course for long in Dermot Deane's office. But she had to call on every bit of self-discipline not to start at the sound of the telephone or let her thoughts wander from the less interesting aspects of her work.

On Tuesday afternoon, just as Mary was thinking almost fretfully that nothing was going to happen *this* day either, Anthea Warrender came into the office. She was looking charming and distinctly prima donna-ish in the kind of simple coat which – Mary knew by now – had probably cost the earth. Supposing that she might well want a private business talk with her employer, Mary gathered up her papers and prepared to depart to the outer office.

But Anthea said, "Don't go, Miss Barlow. This concerns you too. Dermot, Oscar and I are having an informal weekend party at the new house. It's on the Thames, just beyond Windsor, you know. Something between a house-warming and a friendly discussion about future plans. We hope you'll come. And I thought Miss Barlow might like to come too."

While Dermot Deane consulted his desk diary, Anthea turned enquiringly to Mary, who was almost speechless with surprise and joy.

"But, Mrs. Warrender! – why me? It's terribly kind of you even to suggest it, and I can't imagine anything more wonderful, but –"

"Well, we shall be talking over quite a lot of professional stuff and Nick – Nicholas Brenner, you know – said you might be willing to take notes and type out schemes for us. And anyway –" suddenly Anthea smiled her heart-warming, brilliant smile – "Nick says you're a faithful fan of all of us, and that it would probably be a sort of treat for you. Do come. It wouldn't only be a case of our making use of you, you know. We'd really like to have you."

"I can't tell you –" Mary found her voice was husky with emotion and she had to clear her throat. "I can't tell you how much I should love it. Or how much I appreciate your thinking of me like that."

"It was Nick's idea really," Anthea explained. "He says –" her glance rested kindly on Mary – "that you've been a great help to him at this difficult time. And those of us who love Nick are grateful to you for that. He thought – I thought too – it would be nice to give you some pleasure in return. – Well, Dermot?"

"Yes, I can manage it and would like to come," Mary's employer said, making a note in his diary, just as though this were an ordinary engagement and not a passport to paradise.

"Good! Then will you drive Miss Barlow down on Friday evening? You will? – Then we'll expect you both around six."

Mary wished her employer would ask if Suzanne Thomas were coming. But he made no such enquiry, merely thanking Anthea for the invitation while Mary added a few fervent phrases of her own. Then Anthea took her departure and for a minute or two Mary sat there, pretending to work, while gratitude swept over her in great warm waves. Gratitude to Anthea for inviting her, but gratitude to Nicholas too for having so ingeniously arranged that they should spend the weekend together in circumstances no one could scruple to accept.

And she had actually presumed to think he might be planning some cheap little hole-and-corner weekend trip for her!

"I wonder if Suzanne is to be one of the party," said Dermot Deane at that moment.

"I wondered too, and wished rather that you would ask," Mary replied frankly. "It would be nicer without her, wouldn't it?"

"In my view, yes. But they might think she would be amusing for Brenner," said her employer. A possibility which appealed so little to Mary that she could find no comment to make upon it.

He had to go out after that. And, alone in the office,

Mary paused to hug herself and exult afresh over the incredible and glorious thing which had happened. Then, on a sudden bold impulse, she picked up the telephone, dialled the Gloria and asked to speak to Nicholas Brenner.

His voice answered immediately, but not very cordially, and all he said was, "Yes?"

"I just wanted to thank you! Anthea Warrender came in half an hour ago and invited me – and Mr. Deane, of course – to the weekend party. I can't believe it!"

"It's Anthea you have to thank," he said, but she knew from his voice that he was smiling.

"Oh, of course – her too. But she said it was your idea. It's a *wonderful* idea. Was that what you had in mind the other evening, when you said you would think of something for next weekend?"

There was a fractional pause. Then he said, "Not exactly – no, I wasn't quite clear – what you would like. I only knew we'd had enough of restaurants and taxis. The Warrenders are charming hosts. It seemed a good arrangement."

"It couldn't be better," she assured him.

"It will make up for the fact that I can't see you after the performance tomorrow. There's some sort of reception, and we all have to go. It's a bore, but one sometimes has to do these things."

"I hadn't thought of seeing you after the performance anyway," Mary said frankly.

"You hadn't?" He sounded amused and a trifle annoyed. "You do have to be dragged all the way, don't you?"

"All the way where?" Mary wanted to know. But before he could – or chose to – answer that, the other office phone rang, and Mary had to cut short the conversation.

The rest of the week happened to be a very busy time. But even so – and with a recklessness she did not even bother to justify to herself – Mary found time to go shopping, and to spend more on a couple of outfits for the weekend party than she would ordinarily have spent in six months.

She was rewarded by the glance which her employer bestowed on her when he came in late on Friday afternoon to collect her.

"That's nice," he said approvingly. "Eye-catching but in good taste. A difficult combination to achieve." And Mary felt reasonably well prepared for the weekend, even if Suzanne Thomas should be there.

She was not there. And, had Mary known it, Anthea Warrender would have considered it a grave error of judgment to invite her under the same roof as Nicholas Brenner. For all her warmth and charm, Anthea was shrewd. And what she did not know about people by instinct her cynically wide-awake husband had taught her.

"It's really quite a small gathering. Hardly a party at all," she explained to Mary as she took her up to her beautiful room, which looked over the long sloping garden to the river. "Just you and Nick and Dermot, and a couple of very good friends of ours. He's a composer. You may have heard of him – Marcus Bannister –"

"Oh, he wrote 'The Exile', didn't he?"

"Yes, that's right."

"And married the girl who sang the leading role."

"Well, no," Anthea smiled. "As a matter of fact he married the girl who *didn't* get the leading role. At least, she got it at first. And then she stood down, because that marvellous Polish singer, Erna Spolianska, turned up. It was she who absolutely made the first night."

"I remember now. I was thinking he married her –"

"Oh, no! She's a wonderful artist, but not the kind of person you could fit into the Bannister background. The girl he married – a girl called Gail Rostall – is a perfect darling, and very gifted in her own right. In fact –" she stopped. Then she laughed a trifle guiltily and said, "I'm gossiping, I'm afraid."

"Please go on. I'm loving it," Mary assured her, as she stood before the long Venetian mirror, running a comb through her hair.

"Well, Marc has written a second opera, I think with Gail in mind. Oscar considers it as good as 'The Exile' though it's on very different lines, of course. There's a very lovely soprano role that I must say I'd like myself – beautifully lyrical, with a gorgeous aria that's sheer jam for a lyric soprano in the second act. But the work needs an outstanding tenor. And, as I don't need to tell you, outstanding tenors are always pretty thin on the ground. It needs someone romantic-looking with–"

"In fact, Nicholas Brenner?"

"Exactly. So we've got a few wheels within wheels this weekend! We're hoping to interest him. And it wouldn't be a bad idea to have Dermot on our side too. He's a very shrewd judge, you know, and of course quite influential in musical circles. We shan't exactly push anything. But if Nick did like the work – and everything else fell into place – it would be fun, wouldn't it?"

"It would be marvellous." Mary turned from the mirror to cast an approving glance at her hostess. "And the idea of being in at the start of such an enterprise is too thrilling for words. It *was* good of you to ask me too, Mrs. Warrender."

"You seemed the ideal person," Anthea replied frankly.

"Dermot says you're discretion itself. And Nick said he would come if you came too. *Et voilà!*" she laughed.

"Nicholas – Mr. Brenner said that?"

"Yes. I think he showed very good taste," Anthea added lightly, and Mary wondered just what she was thinking.

"This mezzo role you were speaking of –" Mary tried to sound as though she were considering it in a completely artistic sense. "It wouldn't be the kind of role that would interest Suzanne Thomas, for instance? Supposing Gail Bannister didn't want it, I mean."

"She does want it. And Marc wrote it specially for her. In any case, Suzanne wouldn't do at all. It's a fine, rather noble sort of role. Suzanne is a splendid artist in her own individual way, but nobility is not her outstanding characteristic."

Anthea spoke with a calm realism that had no trace of spite in it. And Mary felt so reassured and happy that she was ready to like Gail Bannister on sight.

Later she found no difficulty in living up to this intention, for the composer and his young wife were friendly, easy people to get on terms with. And the only person of whom Mary remained in some considerable awe was her famous host. Warrender, however, could unbend very charmingly in his own home. And if he took no special notice of Mary, at least he was courteous and agreeable to her when he did take note of her existence.

The guest for whom she was waiting came last of all, just before dinner. And although, rather naturally, he did not kiss her in front of the others, he gave her a very special smile as he briefly greeted her.

At dinner, Mary would have been well content to be a listener only as the fascinating professional conversation eddied to and fro around her. But Nicholas drew her in at one point, when audience-reaction was being laughingly discussed.

"You'd better ask Mary about that," he said. "She's a gallery girl. Though, as she claims, one who doesn't actually scream round the stage door."

"She's not the only one here! I was a gallery girl once, come to that," declared Anthea with some pride.

"Were you really?" Mary looked at her and laughed.

"She certainly was," said Warrender unexpectedly. "The very first time I ever took her to Covent Garden – in the director's box, if I remember rightly – she requested me to wave at her friends in the gallery."

"And did you?" asked Mary, fascinated by this sidelight on the conduct of the mighty.

"Certainly."

"With some reluctance. But he did," stated Anthea. "I think that was when I fell in love with you, Oscar. It was so nice of you to understand."

"You're completely mistaken. You simply loathed me then, and as good as told me so," her husband reminded her. "And I wasn't being 'nice'. I was showing off, playing the great man being gracious. You've forgotten."

"Aren't you glad I have the kind of memory which records only the endearing things about you?" Anthea gave him a mischievously sparkling glance.

"Very," he said drily. But he looked at her for a moment in a way that did Mary's romantic heart good.

"Well, if we're all boasting of our gallery days, I too was a gallery girl, of course," remarked Gail Bannister. "And I still like to be up there on a big first night. Were you there on the first night of my husband's opera 'The Exile', Miss Barlow?"

"I certainly was! Were you?"

"No. She was in Germany obstinately singing oratorio," put in her husband. "Just because she felt I ought to have someone else for the leading role."

"She was right too," said Warrender and Dermot Deane in unison.

And — "I think she probably was right," said Mary. "I can't imagine that anyone could have bettered Spolianska." And then, as she saw the chance come pat to her hand, she turned to Marcus Bannister and added, "You'll have to write something else very special for your wife, instead."

"I have done so — I think."

"You *have*? A new opera, you mean?" She was not unaware of the approving glint in Anthea's eyes before she demurely lowered her lashes and looked as though this was not her cue.

"Yes, a new opera. With a role which I think is exactly right for Gail. And —" he smiled down the table at his hostess — "another one which I hope will interest Anthea."

"What about the men?" Mary had no need to simulate interest in that aspect of the work.

"The best role of all is for the tenor," stated Gail without hesitation. "It requires everything — lyrical singing, dramatic acting and a fine figure of a man."

"I hope you recognise yourself, Brenner," remarked Dermot Deane.

"Not really," Nicholas laughed. Then he looked across at the composer. "I take it you've brought the manuscript with you?"

"Of course. One doesn't modestly leave one's brainchild at home on an occasion such as this!"

"In fact —" Nicholas looked round the company and

his glance came to rest on Mary – "this is in the nature of a friendly conspiracy?"

"First thing I've heard of it," said Dermot Deane, disclaiming any involvement.

"The rest of us were in it," Anthea conceded. "Though Mary was a last-minute conspirator. She had to play her part by ear and inspiration. But she certainly brought in the subject of the opera very adroitly."

"Because it was close to her heart, I expect," said Nicholas. And then, as Mary's colour rose, he added carelessly, "She is an opera fan *par excellence*," and her colour ebbed again.

Immediately after dinner Anthea said if they wanted to see the garden and the view across the river before it was dark, they had better go now. So one or two of them strolled out on to the lawn and down towards the river's edge. It was an unusually warm night, with a few early stars hanging low in a deep blue sky. And Mary, making no attempt to pair off with anyone – not even her employer – strolled along beside one of the wide flower borders, enjoying the peace of the scented dusk.

It was only a matter of minutes, however, before she found Nicholas beside her.

"Well, my little conspirator –" he drew her arm through his – "does this weekend still seem a good idea?"

"Wonderful!" She smiled, but without looking at him. "But I wasn't really a conspirator, you know. I heard about the Bannisters' hopes of interesting you, just after I arrived. And I didn't see why I shouldn't introduce the subject of the work for them."

"You disappoint me." He laughed softly. "I hoped you felt you had a personal stake in the game."

"How could I?" She glanced up in frank surprise.

"It's an English opera and a new work. If I took on the leading role that would mean that I stayed in this country a good deal longer than required by my present commitments."

"Oh!" She stopped dead, a great wave of excitement and joy engulfing her. "I hadn't thought of that."

"No?" He bent his head and kissed the side of her cheek. "Well, think of it now."

And then Anthea called from the french window, "Nick! We're going into the studio now. Are you coming?"

They went. Just two of the shadowy figures who converged on the house out of the gathering darkness. But Nicholas had her hand in his until they came into the ring of light thrown from the windows. Then he released her hand, but it seemed to her that the warmth of his clasp remained with her.

To Mary the next hour or two was pure magic. She and her employer – the sole audience – sat at one end of the long studio while the others, with Warrender and Marcus Bannister alternately at the piano, tried over parts of the new work.

"It's got quality," Dermot Deane said once to her. "But then anything with that cast would sound pretty high quality, I reckon."

"What a wonderful voice Gail Bannister has." Mary said that with all sincerity. But something in her told her that she must talk only of Gail and Anthea, otherwise she would be babbling of her love and admiration for Nicholas.

He was wonderful, beyond anything she had yet realised. For one thing, his use of words was something for her to marvel at. Now that he was singing in a language of which she could judge every nuance, she could hear that he used words in the way a great actor does. She murmured something about this, in an academic sort of way, to Dermot Deane.

"Of course, of course," he agreed. "That's part of the secret of his superb singing. Any great musical director or teacher will tell you the same thing – 'Think of the words, think of the words!' That's what helps to colour every musical phrase. I'd like to hear him sing a solo from this work. Anthea says there's a beautiful tenor aria in the first act." And as there was a pause from the group round the piano at this moment, he called out, "Can't we have the tenor solo from the first act?"

"Do you want me to sight-read it?" Nicholas leant forward and took the score from the piano and studied it for a minute or two, humming a little under his breath. "He's telling her the tale, I gather, Marc? Trying to persuade her that he loves her."

"Not quite. More exactly, he's trying to persuade her that *she* loves *him*," Marc corrected with a smile. "She's quite unawakened at this moment. He is sure of his feelings, but not of hers. That's why he says –"

"Yes, yes, I've got it." Nicholas flicked over a page or two. "It seems like a good climax. We'll try it, shall we?"

"Do you want some more light?" Anthea asked.

"No. It's rather effective with just the candles on the piano," Nicholas declared.

"But you can't see the words," protested Anthea. "Nor the notes, come to that."

"I've got the words – here." He tapped his forehead.

"You can't have, in that short space of time!" Anthea was incredulous. "You lucky man! Can you really learn it straight off like that?"

"Yes. I've almost total recall where anything written is concerned," Nicholas explained. "It's just a sort of trick, really. I can't explain it. It's like having perfect pitch, or being able to spot a diamond among the paste. You can either do it or you can't."

"I wish I had the gift!" cried Anthea and Gail in chorus.

"You have other gifts," Nicholas told them, smiling. "Are you ready, Bannister? What is he doing at this point, by the way?"

"Leaning against the wall of the orchard, watching her as she looks from the window into the night."

With completely natural grace Nicholas immediately leant back against the wall behind Marcus, the mellow candlelight softening the strong, handsome lines of his face, in the way the old footlights used to give romantic charm to an actor's expression.

He looked across the piano straight into the darkened room. Straight at Mary. At Dermot Deane too, to tell the truth, but she could not imagine that it was to her employer that those tender, heart-melting phrases were directed. It was to *her*, and her alone, that he was singing them. It was to her that he was saying that she must surely love him, because his love for her was such a real and living force.

"It's not fair!" she thought once, almost drowning in the irresistible sweetness of the moment. "This is meant to be directed at a whole theatreful of people, not just one defenceless girl."

She had forgotten the very existence of her employer by now, of course. She had forgotten about everyone and everything except Nicholas, who in that golden, matchless tenor voice was weaving such a spell of love and enchantment that it was all she could do not to get up and go to him.

At the end everyone broke into spontaneous applause, both for the singer and the song.

"It's an undoubted winner, Bannister." That was Oscar Warrender, shaken out of his habitual professional calm. "It simply can't fail. Particularly if you have Nicholas in the part."

"*Only* if you have Nicholas in the part," murmured Mary.

At which her employer glanced at her and said, "Yes, he certainly knows how to deliver the goods, doesn't he? It almost made me feel myself that I was a silly young girl being serenaded. Partly the effect of his looking straight out of that ring of candlelight at one, of course."

She wanted to say, "You don't suppose he was looking at *you*, do you? He was looking at me. He was singing to me!"

But of course she somehow held her peace. She just joined in the general chorus of approval with a few discreet words. She listened with politeness – and genuine pleasure – to the rest of the excerpts which were tried out. But all through her coursed a sort of warm, golden flood of happiness, because he had sung that love song to her.

Surely, surely he had sung it only for her?

The rest of the evening passed swiftly. Or so it seemed to Mary. Though afterwards she could not recall in any detail what was said or sung. She did remember that Marcus Bannister sat at the piano for some time improvising, while the rest of them relaxed and enjoyed themselves. She had half hoped that Nicholas would come and sit beside her then. But he made no move to do so. And presently good nights were being exchanged and Mary went upstairs, still in a semi-daze of happiness.

She was too excited and moved to go straight to bed. Indeed for the first few minutes she just walked silently up and down her beautiful room, clasping and unclasping her hands. The relief of no longer needing to keep up an appearance of easy composure was such that she simply had to express her feelings in action.

"Theatre people *do* these charming, slightly melo-dramatic things," she told herself once. But the words made almost no real impression upon her.

For a little while longer she heard the sound of voices, the occasional repeated "good night" and the closing of doors. Then silence fell on the house, and only from the open window came the small sounds of night. The twittering of a sleepy bird shifting in the branches of a tree, the cry of a night-owl somewhere in the distance, and the faint lapping of the water as it slid over the little weir at the end of the garden.

Mary switched off all the lights except the one by her bed, and went to sit at the window for a few minutes. Now she was aware of night scents as well as night sounds and, half soothed, half excited by the heavy scent of the clinging roses, she cupped her chin on her hands and gazed out across the garden, her eyes now becoming more accustomed to the darkness, so that she could see the outlines of trees and bushes.

Presently a pale moon came out from behind a cloud, casting a subdued radiance on the path beneath her window. Her thoughts were still formless as her gaze idly followed the moving line of light along the path, until it touched the wall which jutted out at the end. Then, with a sudden start, she realised that the moonlight had touched not only the wall but someone who was standing there.

He was leaning back carelessly against the brick wall, exactly as he had leant back against the studio wall, earlier that evening, and he was looking up at her framed in the subdued light of the one lamp behind her.

"Nicholas –" she hardly breathed the word.

"Come down," he said, softly but in that tone which could carry to the last row of the gallery on little more than a whisper. "It's too beautiful to go to bed yet. Come down, darling."

"I don't think – I don't know –"

"Do you want me to serenade you again?" He had come forward right beneath her window now, and she saw that he was smiling. "I'll make it Faust or Romeo – or Marc's air once more, if that's what you would like."

"No, no," she whispered hastily. "Someone might hear."

"I'd sing pianissimo," he promised, and she heard his laugh. "But if you came down instead –"

"I'm coming – I'm coming!"

"Come through the drawing-room, then. The door on to the terrace is open."

Her hands were shaking a little as she gathered up a soft woollen stole and flung it round her shoulders. Then she slipped quietly out of her room, and went silently down through the silent house.

CHAPTER V

As Mary stepped out on to the terrace she saw that he was standing there in the moonlight, like a figure on a stage, and he held out his arms to her. Without even pausing to think what she was doing or what this might imply, she ran straight into his arms. And as he held her and kissed her she made only a fugitive clutch at her vanishing common sense.

"Nicholas, this is crazy! I don't know what we think we're doing –"

"I know exactly what *I* am doing," he retorted gaily. "I'm kissing the girl I love, and enjoying every minute of it."

She was silent then, quite still in the circle of his arms. He had actually said she was the girl he loved! But just how much he meant by that she simply did not know.

Presently, impelled by the pressure of the arm he kept round her, she went slowly down the few steps with him to the lawn. Perhaps by accident or perhaps with the intention of avoiding any chance observation from the house, they kept mostly to the patches of heavy shadow cast by the trees on either side of the garden, and for a while they strolled in silence.

Then he said at last, "You knew I sang that song to you, didn't you?"

"I hoped you did. But Dermot Deane thought you were singing it to him —" there was a little catch of laughter in her voice — "so afterwards I told myself perhaps that was just the way you worked your special magic. Making everyone in your audience feel, 'He's singing that to *me*.' "

"I was not singing it to Dermot Deane," he assured her gravely.

At which she laughed softly again and said, "It's a perfectly beautiful air, isn't it?" and she tried to sound as though she were academically considering the song rather than the singer.

"It seemed to me one of the great tunes of the world. But perhaps that was partly due to the circumstances in which I sang it." He was silent for a moment, then he said abruptly, "Do you want me to take the role, Mary?"

"I?" She checked a moment in her slow walk and then went on again. "Of course I want you to take it if you would like to — if you think it's the right thing for your career."

"I didn't mean that."

"No?" She hoped he could not feel that she trembled slightly. "What did you mean?"

"Do you want me to have a good reason for staying on much longer in London?" he asked deliberately.

She was silent, making a tremendous effort to suppress her instinct to cry out, "Of course I do! I can't even bear to think of your leaving."

Desperately she tried to recall the sensible things she had said to herself not a week ago, in her own bedroom. All about facing the fact that he couldn't mean anything serious in her life, and that therefore she had better draw back from this entanglement before she was badly hurt.

But then there was such a thing as not caring about

being hurt later. Later seemed such a long way away! At the moment all she could think of was that he wanted her to say the simple truth – that every day he stayed longer would be precious to her.

"Well?" he said quietly, and she realised that she must have been silent for several moments.

There were so many ways of answering, of course. She could refuse to have the responsibility of choosing for him. She could say airily that naturally one liked one's operatic favourites to be around for as long as possible. She could say she liked the work and wanted to hear it done in the best possible way. She could say –

Mary said none of these things. She gave no qualifying reason at all. She merely said, in a half whisper, "I should like you to stay as long as possible in London."

"Thank you, darling." She felt him very lightly kiss the side of her cheek again. "Tell me something. How much of that admission was addressed to the famous tenor, and how much to me – Nicholas?"

"I don't know!" suddenly she panicked. "Do I *have* to say?"

"Not if you don't want to." He was quite gentle about that. A little sombre perhaps, as befitted an operatic hero at a display of indecision on the part of the heroine. But he was not insistent.

"I must go in now," she exclaimed, not even sure why she felt they had said all that could be said at that moment. But he seemed to understand. – Or was it just that his artistic timing was always superb?

Quite unbidden, that disquieting thought flicked across her consciousness. She wished she could have kept it away. No hint of cynicism should have clouded the brightness of this experience. But something deep inside her made her hurry that last good night, so that she almost fled from him, across the terrace and into the darkened house again.

At first she could not even grope her way. She stood irresolute, hearing only the thumping of her own heart. Then her eyes adjusted to the indoor darkness, and she felt her way more surely through the long drawing-room and out into the hall.

There was a dim light on the wide staircase. She had been glad of it when she was coming down. She was even more glad of it now. In some strange way, it seemed to light the way not only to her room, but back to the commonsense safety of her own way of life. Nothing in the remotest degree dangerous had happened in those ten or fifteen minutes with Nicholas in the garden. And yet she felt that those few words which they had exchanged had somehow breeched the walls which surrounded the conventional life of the Mary Barlow she had always known.

In that moment, she would almost have been glad to be no more than the carefree fan she had once been. Someone who gazed happily at her stars from a distance and romanced about them harmlessly. To be involved with them personally was something totally different.

It was when Nicholas had asked her how much he was the famous tenor to her and how much the man that a sort of warning bell had sounded. And like an echo had come the other, even more disquieting question: How much of *his* attitude related to the man, and how much was he the fine artist playing his role almost unconsciously?

It was a thought which followed her into her sleep and did not entirely leave her for the rest of that weekend.

For the others, of course, the weekend had already served its delightful purpose. Dermot Deane had been successfully interested in Marc Bannister's opera, and Nicholas was willingly committed to singing in it. There was nothing to do but enlarge on this pleasing conclusion, and conversation tended to centre round the possibilities of a future production in the fairly near future.

Though the work had not been actually commissioned for the Opera House, Oscar Warrender was confident that a space would be found for it in the coming season. And as Mary listened – and took occasional notes for them all – she realised that Nicholas was evidently planning on making London his headquarters for some while.

"There's a good deal else offering, now that people realise you're in operatic circulation again," objected Dermot Deane, who naturally saw things from the point of view of the agent and impresario who preferred his clients to spread their professional wings as far as possible.

"You could do the early study on this work almost anywhere. And, much though we like to have you around, there are several managers clamouring for you."

"If I'm going to do this role I'd like the opportunity of some early study with the composer," replied Nicholas coolly. "It's not often a singer gets such a chance. The other places can wait."

"Not all of them!" Dermot Deane protested.

"Not all, perhaps. But first things first. Let me have a copy of the score when you can, Marc. I've only the Lenskys on my plate at the moment."

Dermot Deane started to say something about a short Continental concert tour – which was news to Mary – but Nicholas frowned.

"Not just now," he said curtly. "We'll discuss that later." And the subject was dropped.

To Mary, who felt her whole life had changed since

last night, it seemed incredible that the rest of the week-end could pass in such leisurely tranquillity. Discussion of a mere opera might be of immense importance to the others – even, apparently to Nicholas. But she was concerned with real life – *her* life – and not with some stage situation.

She hardly knew what it was she expected Nicholas to do or say. But surely one could not have a declaration of love – even a half laughing one – and just go on from there as though everything were as it had been before?

It was true that there were other people around them most of the time. But if he had really wanted to have her to himself, he could surely have found an opportunity. Or *made* an opportunity, come to that. She wished now, passionately, that she had not refused to answer his leading question, and she wondered unhappily if by her stupid moment of panic and indecision she had spoiled that indefinable bond between them.

To her disappointment, Nicholas left rather early on the Sunday afternoon, in company with the Bannisters, who had persuaded him to stop off for twenty-four hours at their own small home in Sussex. She hoped it was not just her imagination that, as the good-byes were said, he held her hand a fraction longer than was necessary.

Certainly he said that he would see her at the first night of "Eugene Onegin" on the Thursday, and added, "I'll have your ticket left at the box office in my name."

It comforted her a little to remember his insisting that he wanted her downstairs because he could see her there. But then she had to watch him go off so deep in conversation with Marc Bannister that he even forgot to look back.

Was that how dedicated artists were when it came to

their art? With all else forgotten or pushed aside? In theory, this had always seemed to her a very proper and praiseworthy attitude. In practice, it was curiously unacceptable.

Mary drove back to town with her employer, telling herself as she had told Anthea Warrender – that she had had a wonderful time. She had, of course! Who could share a weekend with those charming and celebrated people and not feel that it had been an experience in a thousand?

But as she went over each detail of the weekend in her mind, she felt that all the highlights had come in the very first evening. And she wondered if she had herself been responsible for the slight dimming of the radiance thereafter.

No one suggested that she should go to the dress rehearsal of "Eugene Onegin" on Tuesday, but at least she knew that Nicholas must be back in town again. If she had followed her most slavish inclination she would more or less have sat by the telephone, waiting for him to call. But she rallied her self-respect and good sense, and when Barry phoned, pressing her to go out with him that evening, she went.

Again she had the curious feeling that it was almost a relief to go with Barry because he presented no problems. And this time she was sharply aware that this was her reaction, and she soberly accepted the implications of it.

Perhaps this was how sensible girls saw things, in the end. Perhaps they thought of the improbable glamour of certain brief experiences as outside the natural scheme of existence, and settled for the familiar – as regards both events and people.

The idea was confusing. Not least because Barry had

himself once represented glamour and the almost unattainable. Now, in contrast to Nicholas Brenner and his world, Barry seemed — not ordinary — but understandable and unproblematical, in a wholly reassuring manner.

He collected her from the office in an attractive car she had not seen before.

"Barry, how lovely! Is it yours?" And when he nodded smilingly, she added, "I didn't know you were thinking of a new car. The old one looked all right to me."

"Did it?" He was still smiling as he looked ahead. "We're celebrating this evening, my love. I've had a pretty staggering promotion, the kind of step-up that I hadn't expected for at least a couple of years."

"Oh, Barry, I *am* pleased! Where are we going to celebrate?" she asked.

"At a charming place I discovered recently, just beyond Windsor."

"Just — beyond Windsor?" She thought there must be an odd note in her voice, but he didn't appear to have heard it.

"Yes. A glorified riverside pub, with a beautiful outlook over the river. The kind of place for a real celebration."

She thought of the Warrenders' place "just beyond Windsor", where she had spent that weekend of mingled magic and disappointment, and the garden, sloping down to the river, where she had walked in the moonlight with Nicholas. But she could not talk lightly to Barry — or indeed anyone else — of that experience. So she just said that it sounded delightful, and left it at that.

Barry had telephoned beforehand, it seemed, and a table had been reserved for them on the balcony, overlooking a stretch of river and country which seemed both excitingly and disturbingly familiar to Mary. They were on the opposite side of the river from the Warrenders' house, but almost within sight of it. And to Mary, in her present mood, there seemed to be something almost symbolical about this. It was as though the smoothly flowing river divided the two sides of her life from each other.

Here, with Barry, she was in familiar, almost conventional territory. On the other side lay that magical, disturbing world where people and events were over life-size. It was fascinating, it was breathtaking. But it was alien.

Or at least, it always had been so.

In Barry's company it was inconceivable to believe that a famous tenor had stood beneath her window, offered laughingly to serenade her, and made her come down into the moonlight where she had run willingly into his arms. And yet, just across the river, that was exactly what had happened.

It was like something one invented to oneself but never really believed in. But to her it had happened. To her, Mary Barlow, who was now sitting opposite Barry Courtland, enjoying a most excellent dinner, in celebration of his having had a sensational promotion in his office.

Not until they were lingering pleasantly over their coffee did he say, "I suppose you know why I brought you here, Mary?"

"Why, to celebrate your promotion, of course." She brought her wandering glance back from across the river and smiled as she raised her liqueur glass to him. "Congratulations, Barry dear. And may this be the first of many."

"Many promotions or many shared celebrations?"

"Both, I suppose," she said lightly.

"That argues that we would be together," he pointed

108

out deliberately. "That *my* promotions would be a reason for *us* to celebrate together. Mary, is that how you would like it to be?" He reached for her hand and held it although she made a slight instinctive effort to withdraw it.

"I wasn't thinking!" she said quickly. "Of course I should always be glad of anything nice which happened to you, but—"

"Don't let's talk around the point," he interrupted. "No man likes to admit he was a fool, but there are times when he should do so. I was a fool to turn my back on you, Mary, and go after Elspeth. I know it now."

"Oh, please!"

"It's true. I'm not criticising her, I'm criticising myself. I'd give a lot to be able to put back the clock to where we were a year or more ago. But no one gets a chance to do that. Maybe no one deserves that kind of chance. But I'm saying now what I should have said long ago. It's you I love, Mary, and it's you I want to marry. At least by waiting until now I can offer you a great deal more than I ever had before."

"Barry dear, I don't know what to say to you." She felt distressed and guilty that she had let him go so far without her realising and somehow heading him off. "But it's true — what you said about one not being able to put back the clock. Things have changed. *We* have changed—" she stopped, unable to define her feelings or her position further.

"You mean you can't forget the shabby way I treated you."

"No! I don't mean that at all. It hurt at the time, of course — I was more naïve and vulnerable then. Perhaps I rather asked to be hurt, and it wasn't just your fault. But — it happened. And whatever there was between us —

went. It *had* to. You were engaged — pretty well married — to another girl. I did my best to forget, to detach my feelings. Then life went on. Things — changed." She repeated the rather futile explanation, hoping he would somehow accept this very general plea.

He did not. He looked straight at her and said, "You mean, of course, that you think you're in love with Nicholas Brenner."

"What makes you say that?"

"The way you've behaved — spoken of him — ever since I've seen you again. At first I thought your — your remoteness towards me was something to do with my own behaviour. You'd have been justified, and I'd have been almost relieved if that had been the case. But it isn't that at all. It's that you're dazzled by sudden contact with the kind of person who is right outside your usual orbit."

She was silent, pushing a few crumbs about the table-cloth and studying them with unnecessary attention.

"Look, my dear — I don't want to plead my own cause by running down another fellow. But it would never work, you know."

"What wouldn't?" She glanced up quickly.

"Anything between you and Brenner. Even if he wanted to marry you — and I don't believe you're any too sure of that — it wouldn't be the right life for you. All that stagey glamour, that artificial setting —"

"You don't know," she interrupted in a low voice. "There's a side of him which is almost touchingly simple. He doesn't live all the time in the limelight. He doesn't want to."

"Not all the time — no." Barry's tone was determinedly reasonable. "But part of him — the greater part — is a public figure. In addition, he is truly what's meant by a

110

dedicated artist, I'll give him that. You are an ordinary girl. In the dearest and most valuable sense of the word, you're an ordinary girl. You would want the ordinary things. You – and they – just wouldn't count, Mary, if you stood in the way of his art. That's the way these people are. Think very carefully, my dear. I don't know how far things have gone –"

He paused, but she didn't offer to tell him. For one thing, she simply did not know herself. And after a moment Barry went on.

"I'm not trying to be argumentative about someone you obviously like very much. And I see I chose the wrong time to tell you I love you and want to marry you. Forget about that for the moment, if you'd rather. I shan't press things or make myself a nuisance. But just remember I'm your friend, and I'm there if you want me. And now –" he glanced at his watch – "it's time I took you home."

She knew he was behaving very well. Even her mother could not have faulted his conduct on this occasion. And she wished she could have told him she was grateful to him and was sorry she had spoiled his celebration mood. But what could she do? She could not conscientiously allow any sort of tender situation to develop between them. At the same time, nor could she state that she intended to marry Nicholas Brenner.

For the very good reason that she was not at all sure if Nicholas intended to marry *her*.

It said something for Barry's social skill that he somehow contrived to make that return journey normal and unembarrassing. But Mary was thankful beyond expression when he finally deposited her at her own front door.

Her mother was not yet in bed and, having misunderstood Mary's telephone message from the office, was under the impression that she had been out with Nicholas Brenner again.

"Oh, no!" Mary exclaimed when she realised her mother's mistake. "I went out with Barry. And don't look blank like that, Mother. He behaved exceptionally well."

"In what way?" enquired Mrs. Barlow with some interest.

"Well —" Mary hesitated. Then, because she simply had to tell someone, and she knew her mother for a discreet and sensible confidante, she burst out, "He asked me to marry him, and I refused him. I — had to."

"Why did you 'have' to, my dear? Not that I would blame you, after the way he —"

"It's not that! It's not that at all. I'm in love with someone else," Mary said, and she drew a long sigh of relief at being able to admit this to someone at last.

"Oh, dear —" her mother rubbed the bridge of her nose thoughtfully, a trick she had when she was a little disturbed. "I suppose you've been losing your head over that singer."

Put that way, it did not sound quite like the love story of the century. More as though Mary had been eating too many sweets. She dropped into a low chair and ran her hands through her hair rather distractedly.

"I suppose I have," she admitted. "Barry says —"

"Oh, you discussed it with Barry?" Her mother looked surprised.

"Yes." Mary was rather surprised herself, now she came to think of it, for Barry was not somehow cast for the faithful old friend in whom one confided. "Like you, he had guessed that I was — am — in love with Nicholas."

"Does Nicholas guess too?"

"Nicholas knows — I think. And he says he loves me.

112

But I don't know, Mother, whether it's partly just a romantic piece of play-acting with him, or whether it's the real thing. I *want* it to be the real thing, and sometimes I'm almost sure it is. But he's not like anyone else I've ever known. I suppose that's why I feel in such an emotional turmoil. I'm sorry to worry you with all this –"

"That's what mothers are for," said Mrs. Barlow kindly. "There isn't anything to be ashamed of in not knowing your own mind at this point, and probably I'm the best person for you to try out your theories on. But there's one thing –" she paused, as though choosing her next words carefully.

"Yes, Mother?"

"If it did work out as you think you want it, and you married this very famous man, there would be a lot of problems in that kind of life which you've never had to tackle before, you know."

"That's what Barry said."

"Barry isn't exactly a disinterested party," replied her mother crisply. "Nor am I, of course. I'm thinking only of your good, which is how it should be. You won't want advice, even from me. People always say they want advice, but they don't. They only want someone to tell them what they want to hear. But remember this, Mary – it's very seldom enough just to love a man. You have to like him too, and like his kind of life. If you don't, there's a great deal of painful adjusting to be done. It has been done, but not very often, and none of it comes easily. Now you'd better go to bed, dear. You look all washed out. And you still have to go to the office in the morning, even if you can't decide whom to marry."

Mary laughed a little and kissed her mother good night. Some people, she knew, would have found this dry, commonsense way of talking rather unsympathetic. But she liked it. It did her more good than any amount of sentimental sympathising, and she went to bed oddly comforted. Even though her mother – who disagreed with Barry on many points – had undoubtedly agreed with him on one conclusion: That if she married Nicholas, life would not be particularly easy for her.

This sober reflection remained with her the next day and quite a large part of Thursday. It deserted her entirely when Nicholas came on to the stage as Lensky in "Eugene Onegin".

She remembered immediately his laughing remark that he rather fancied himself in the caped coat and tall hat of the period, and she thought she had never seen him look so handsome. Even before he began to sing, her heart was his all over again. And when, in addition to everything else, there was that beguiling, heart-searching voice, she forgot about any doubts – expressed or otherwise.

At one point she was nearly sure he saw her, sitting there in the second row, though of course he was far too professional to give the slightest sign that he did. He was absorbed in his part, playing it with a charm and elegance that were entirely characteristic. And when, in the final moments of Lensky's life – just before his death in the duel – he sang with a sort of contemplative melancholy the beautiful aria allotted to him, Mary could hardly restrain her tears.

It was when he was taking a curtain call after the scene that he unmistakably picked her out in the audience and gave her a brilliant smile all to herself. After that, the rest of the opera meant little to Mary, who secretly thought Onegin himself a bit of a bore and in no way to be compared with Lensky.

Afterwards she went round. Nowadays she had fewer qualms when she presented herself at the stage door, and there was no query at all about her going up to his dressing-room. In some indefinable way, she had acquired the status of those who GO IN.

He was alone in his dressing-room when she came and, having had nothing to do in the last act, he had already changed and was ready to go. But, just as he reached for his coat, he hesitated and then spoke over his shoulder to her, with an odd touch of something like nervousness which she had never seen in him before.

"There's something for you on the dressing-table, Mary. I hope you like it."

"Something for me? – where?" She looked at the dressing-table which seemed unnaturally tidy now that all the make-up had been cleared from it. And all she could see was a small and very beautiful little leather case which quite obviously contained a ring.

"There – the ring." He spoke almost impatiently.

"A – ring?" She picked up the case slowly. "For me?"

"For you, darling. If you will take it." He came behind her then and put his arms round her, so that she could see the reflection of him in the mirror as he smiled at her over her shoulder. "It's your engagement ring."

"*Nicholas!*"

She snapped open the case, and every light in the small, overheated room seem to flash from the one superb diamond.

"Nicholas –" she said again, more softly. And it was not only the brilliance of the diamond which dazzled her. It was his smile, the feel of his arms around her, the incredible, wonderful, shattering discovery that he did indeed love her and want to marry her.

Nothing which her mother or Barry had said could matter now. The whole world contained only one all-embracing truth. Nicholas loved her.

"Do you like it?" He put his cheek against hers and looked at her in the mirror.

"I – love it," she said huskily. "There's never been a ring like it before. Never!"

"And do you love me too?"

"You know I do!" She turned in his arms, so that she was facing him and could kiss him.

"No, I didn't know," he told her with a laugh. "At least, not absolutely. You seemed suddenly so doubtful yourself, that night on the terrace. I felt I'd stampeded you – got my timing wrong somehow."

"Don't talk about 'timing'," she exclaimed reproachfully, "as though it were a theatrical scene. It was real, wasn't it? It was real?"

"My darling, of course it was real!" He looked astonished, even a little shocked. "I suppose the words of one's profession come naturally to one's lips."

"Of course, of course," she said eagerly. And then she held out her hand, the fingers widespread, so that he could put on her ring for her.

He kissed her hand, when the ring was firmly there, and asked, "When are you going to marry me?"

"Whenever you say – I think." She smiled. "I should have to give some decent period of notice to Dermot Deane, of course –"

"And I shall have to do that concert tour first."

"Have you got a concert tour?" She looked surprised. "Where? In this country?" She thought how she would love to hear him in concert.

"No. Holland and Germany. One in Amsterdam, one

116

in The Hague and three or four in Germany. The whole thing won't take longer than three weeks. And not much preparation needed. We've done the same sort of thing before."

"We? You mean they're joint recitals with someone?"

"With Suzanne – yes. There's quite a vogue for joint recitals at the moment, usually husband and wife teams."

Mary felt suddenly as though a supply of air had been cut off.

"You mean – Suzanne Thomas?" She enunciated rather slowly and carefully, so that he should not guess she was nearly choking with rage and dismay.

"Yes, of course. As you know, we work well together," he said. "Shall we go now? I'm starving, aren't you?"

CHAPTER VI

No possible answer came to Mary's mind at that moment. Only furious half-sentences, expressing her utter repudiation of this ridiculous idea that Nicholas should go on a concert tour with Suzanne Thomas.

Suzanne, who hardly bothered to conceal the fact that she found him eminently desirable as a companion, a colleague – a lover, if he were so inclined. It was impossible that Nicholas – an experienced artist and surely a man of the world – could suppose Suzanne would not take this heaven-sent opportunity of drawing her net more tightly round him.

Apparently completely unaware of the tempest of feeling which had struck Mary, Nicholas was already holding open the dressing-room door for her. And there was nothing to do but pass out into the narrow corridor and down the stone steps to the stage door.

One or two people called out, "Good night," as they went, which saved Mary from having to make any real conversation. She was getting her breath back now. And with it a certain degree of natural composure. She would have to talk to him, of course. Reasonably, affectionately, but quite emphatically. He *could* not go on this tour with Suzanne.

It was not as though a whole company were going. It

would be just the two of them. An accompanist too, presumably. Though Mary could well imagine how easily Suzanne would get rid of a mere accompanist when his or her services were not required. Most of the time it would be just Nicholas and Suzanne. In Amsterdam, in The Hague, in this and that German city. Feted and admired, coupled together wherever they went. Hadn't Nicholas himself said carelessly that most of these joint recitals were undertaken by husband and wife teams?

That he could *say* such a thing to her and not realise that an unwelcome shock it must be!

He was not a stupid man. Until this moment she had not supposed him to be an insensitive one. It was just — it *must* be just — that once he was involved in his artistic and professional career, nothing and no one else mattered.

Just as Barry had said!

As the shock of Barry's remembered words hit her afresh they reached the stage door where, inevitably, a large crowd was waiting. With an immense effort Mary forced a calm and smiling expression to her face. She stood in the doorway, waiting while Nicholas autographed a few programmes. And, as she did so, she suddenly remembered — with an even greater shock, if possible — how that golden girl, Nicholas's wife Monica, had stood in that very same doorway, smiling as though she had not a care in the world.

And all the time, if report were correct, she too must have been consumed by jealous frustration.

Was *that* the life of a famous singer's wife? Had she already been thrown in at the deep end? With the absolute necessity of concealing her feelings, even though they went as deep as human feelings could go? This evening should have been the most radiant and cloudless of

119

her whole life. This was the evening when Nicholas had asked her to marry him. And yet, within minutes of her accepting him and realising that she was the happiest girl in the world, she was being torn to pieces with fear and dismay.

"It must be some lack in *me*," she told herself. "It's my own fault. The very fact that he was so frank about it all shows there's nothing — absolutely nothing — for me to be worried about."

That thought did bring a measure of relief and consolation. And, in the car, with Nicholas's arm round her and his lips against her cheek, she was almost convinced that everything was all right. Of *course* it was all right. Certainly insofar as he loved *her* and not Suzanne Thomas or anyone else.

What was frightening was the unknown factor of Suzanne's power, once she had the scene entirely to herself. That she wanted Nicholas for herself was something Mary knew instinctively to the very roots of her being.

"But one must trust the man one loves," she told herself desperately. "Am I to start by thinking I can't let him out of my sight? How paltry! How small-minded and stupid."

But — Suzanne. That was the rub! Suzanne, of all people.

"What's the matter, darling?" Nicholas asked at that moment. "You're so very quiet."

"Am I?" Even to her own ears her laugh sounded faintly artificial. "I'm still just trying to believe that all this has really happened."

But the moment she had said that she felt her heart sore and heavy with the realisation that she was already telling him less than the truth. Her whole being revolted against such an idea, and she knew she could not possibly start life with Nicholas like this.

"It isn't only that." She took a grip on her courage and strove to make her voice sound as quiet and unprovocative as possible. "It's – do you *have* to do this concert tour with Suzanne?"

There was only a fractional pause before his reply, but she knew instantly that, whatever shock she had received this evening, she had administered a chilling one in return.

"Yes, I do." His tone was very cool. "I've already signed the contract and so has she. Why?"

He sounded like a stranger all at once. And, as she stared at the impassive back of the hired chauffeur, beyond the glass panel of the car, it occurred to her that it was as though a glass panel had suddenly arisen between her and Nicholas too. And then she remembered that not only had Monica suffered this kind of jealousy; she had made their married life a hell because of it.

In that moment Mary jettisoned the exact truth without scruple. And, like someone slipping down a cliff to disaster, she clutched frantically at the one thing which could check the descent.

"Because I just don't know how I'm going to do without you for three whole weeks." She touched his hand tenderly. "What else?"

"Oh, darling!" He caught her in his arms and held her close in what she knew was an access of relief as well as love. "Forgive me! For a moment I thought – I forget you're so different –"

And she managed to ask gently, "What did you think, Nicholas?"

"It's ridiculous to have this obsessive fear! I thought for a moment that you were jealous."

He had thought – but for a moment only – that she was jealous!

"You see, Monica, poor girl, was jealous of everyone and everything. She checked my every expression, every reaction – sometimes, I felt, my every thought. She even used other people –" he gave a distasteful little shudder – "her so-called friends. She would ask, say, someone in the chorus who was flattered by her attention to spy on me and report on my attitude to my women colleagues. In the end it almost destroyed both of us."

There was a moment of appalled silence in which Mary found herself holding his hand tightly, as though only by touch could she draw him back from that remembered abyss of horror. Then he gave a shamefaced little laugh and exclaimed, "I was a fool to think it could happen again. With you, of all people."

"I won't even *use* the word 'jealous'," she promised eagerly. Then, anxious to catch his lighter mood, she added, "Though I was going to say I should be jealous of all those lucky people listening to your recitals while I was in London working for Dermot Deane."

"It won't be for long," he reminded her smilingly. "Once we're married you'll come with me everywhere."

It was true, of course. Once they were married. The very words brought a flood of relief and consolation. She was to be his wife – his *wife*! How then could she possibly indulge in petty jealousy and fear, just because he would be away from her for three weeks?

With Suzanne Thomas, of course – that was the point. But she simply would not think about that. Suppose it had been Anthea Warrender, for instance –

Oh, if only it *had* been dear, safe, loyal Anthea Warrender, who adored her own husband and never looked at another man! But it was not, and one must accept the fact.

Over supper she managed to drive her fears into the farthest corner of her mind, so that even she hardly knew they were there. And as Nicholas and she discussed the future and made tentative plans, the wonderful reality of it all began to take shape, and her fears seemed proportionately foolish and unimportant.

They agreed that there should be no public announcement of their engagement for the moment. On Nicholas's side, he had an almost morbid dislike of the kind of publicity which attended the romantic affairs of a popular star. And, for her part, Mary thought she would like some time in which to make the adjustment between her present quiet life and the future which was going to take a lot of getting used to.

"I shall tell my parents, of course –"

"But of course!" Nicholas seemed rather shocked at any other idea, which she found endearing. "And I must come and make myself known to them. I hope they'll like me." He sounded quite gravely concerned about that.

"Mother will," Mary said positively. "It will take my father a bit longer to accept the idea that his well-loved but ordinary daughter could possibly make a success of marrying a famous opera star."

"Will he really look at it that way?" Nicholas smiled, intrigued but slightly mystified.

"Of course. Lots of people – my sort of people – will see it in that way too. I suppose even Dermot Deané –"

"Ah – Dermot Deane." Nicholas looked considering. "You say you'll have to give him notice before you leave?"

"Why, certainly! A month at least. Is there any objection to that?"

"I'd rather he didn't know about us too early. The impresario side of him simply wouldn't be able to resist the publicity implications. However much we insisted that we preferred to keep our private affairs private, he would be bound to drop a hint here and there. And that sort of thing goes round our particular world like wildfire."

"Do you think –" Mary turned her beautiful ring on her finger – "it would be better to say nothing to *anyone* until you come back from your concert tour?"

The moment she had said that she wondered if she had made a grave error. For surely the sooner the position was made clear to Suzanne, the better.

So she said quickly, trying to make her tone completely casual,

"You could tell Suzanne, of course."

"My dear!" he laughed. "Suzanne least of all. She's an arrant gossip and would tell everyone, if only to show that she knew my affairs better than anyone else."

It was not said in a tone of harsh criticism. But even mild criticism of Suzanne from such a quarter fell sweetly on Mary's ear at the moment, and suddenly she felt happier and more confident than she had at any time since she first heard of the tour.

"Well then," she said expansively, "let's make no exceptions at all. I won't even tell my parents, unless I feel I just can't bear not to. It isn't as though we have to wait long. You'll be going on this tour – when?"

"The twenty-first of this month. We shall be back by the middle of September. You can give your notice in to Dermot at the end of August or beginning of September, telling him to keep his mouth shut until I return. He won't do so entirely, but –"

"I'll just say I'm getting married. I needn't tell him it's you."

"He'll guess."

"Oh, Nicholas, why should he?"

"Because he has that sort of nose. He can smell good news a mile away and bad news two miles away. That's why he's a successful impresario."

Mary laughed.

"Anyway, if you have to tell him at that point, it won't matter. I shall be back a couple of weeks later, and we can be married at the end of September."

When he actually put a date to it Mary felt it was no dream, after all. This improbable, romantic, wonderful thing really was going to happen to her. To her, Mary Barlow, who not so long ago had thought it the height of bliss just to sit in the gallery at the Opera House and listen to Nicholas Brenner singing on the stage.

Before they left the restaurant she suggested that perhaps he should keep her ring for her until the engagement was made public. But he would not hear of it.

"No, my darling. It's yours – now and for ever. Take it home and hide it if you like. Or show it to your mother. I still think she should be told. But don't try to return it to me for so much as a day! It would be unlucky."

"Oh, Nicholas, are you as superstitious as that?"

"Of course. All stage people have their little superstitions. In addition, I'm partly Slav, remember, which makes me even worse." He laughed and touched her hand lightly. "You're marrying quite a difficult fellow in many ways. Did you know that?"

She did. But she found no problem in smiling back at him and saying she would have chosen no one else.

To this idea she clung during the next rather difficult days. Like all engaged girls, she longed to tell everyone of her happiness and good fortune. And up to now she had lived in a world where this would have been the most natural thing to do. It was hard to accept a situation in which one's simplest private action might have unwelcome public results, and to Mary, who was by nature open-hearted and impulsive, the necessary restrictions were very irksome.

Most trying of all was to have to pretend, in the office, that Nicholas was no more to her than any other artist they handled. Her employer was inclined to talk frankly to her, for he had already found that he could do this with safety. And he was even beginning occasionally to ask her opinion of this or that performer.

"You've got innate taste," he told her approvingly, "which is something you can't teach or learn. Clever of you to spot that Middleton is a performer rather than a real music-maker. And I think you're right when you say that little French coloratura will go far if she will accept soubrette roles and not fancy herself as Violetta or Gilda. One of these days I'll send you out to make a spot judgment on your own. You could be a lot of help to me if I could come to rely on that side of your work."

Mary was pleased, as well she might be, when he said this. But she was not so pleased when he went on to ask outright, "What do you think of Brenner and Suzanne teaming up for this concert tour? They could make quite a big thing of it if they wanted to. They complement each other quite extraordinarily, both artistically and vocally. And incidentally, they look remarkably good on a platform together."

"They've done it before, haven't they?" Mary asked, in order to avoid expressing an opinion.

"Yes. In Canada on one occasion. Suzanne was on her home ground there, and that made her a very useful part-

126

ner for him. That was in Monica's time, of course. I think she made difficulties. She usually did, to tell the truth. Now there wouldn't be *that* problem at any rate."

"No," agreed Mary, but she felt her mouth go dry.

Dermot Deane was in a gossipy mood. He leaned back in his chair, smiled reflectively and said, "I wonder if he'll marry her? She's going to mount a pretty powerful campaign, if I'm not much mistaken."

(And Nicholas had said he could smell bad news two miles off!)

"I don't think they'd suit each other," she said coldly, because she had to say something.

"No? Well, she's not everyone's cup of tea, of course. Not mine, for one. But she's genuinely fond of him in her way, and he's used to having a managing woman around. Monica conditioned him to that. Suzanne is a tremendous go-getter, both for herself and those she likes. She could be quite an asset in his career."

"But hardly much comfort to him personally! I should think he's tired of having a managing woman around, as you put it."

"Could be." Deane's reflective glance rested on her for a moment, which made her uncomfortable. "That's probably why he has enjoyed your company from time to time."

Mary produced what she hoped was a non-committal smile and went on determinedly with her work.

But she checked in the easy flow of her typing when her employer capped the conversation with the philosophical remark:

"Well, this tour will be the test, I expect. She'll have him to herself, and she'll make the most of her opportunities, if I know my Suzanne."

127

"Don't you think it was a mistake to encourage them to arrange this tour, then?" demanded Mary, and her suppressed agitation made that sound almost aggressive. "You *know* she couldn't possibly make him happy. If he's going to marry again, wouldn't it be much better that he –"

"My dear girl!" Dermot Deane had let her get thus far out of sheer astonishment, but he interrupted her now with a genuinely amused laugh. "I don't undertake to look after my clients' private affairs. I'm growing grey and bald in the service of their professional ones. That's enough for me. If Brenner likes to fool around with Suzanne Thomas, who am I to take a dangerous hand? He must look after himself."

"But suppose he made another disastrous marriage and was miserable? Wouldn't that affect his work and career – and incidentally you?"

"Not necessarily. Some of them do their best work when they're in an emotional crises," replied Dermot Deane callously. "There's no hard and fast rule about these things. That's why it's almost always best to let them take their natural course."

He seemed to think that really did conclude the discussion. But for the next three minutes at least Mary quite hated her good-natured, cynical employer.

Afterwards she assured herself that it was just the way he talked. He enjoyed throwing off these verbal fireworks in the privacy of his own office. They made up for his having to be super discreet outside. He didn't really believe half he himself said. Or did he? and he was probably quite wrong in this particular case. He *must* be.

Even so, the few weeks before Nicholas went off on his tour were anything but unalloyed happiness to the girl he

128

was going to marry. When she was with him, everything was clear and beautiful and even reassuring. It seemed then both ridiculous and unworthy to suppose that anyone could threaten her position.

But there were so many times when she was not with him, when he was deeply involved with his work.

There must, she knew, be long discussions and intensive rehearsals with Suzanne. They were not, either of them, the kind of people to throw on a performance and expect all to go well on the night. They were both intensely professional, artistically dedicated, and absolute perfectionists. It was no wonder that they had such profound appreciation of each other as colleagues.

So long as it was as colleagues, well and good. But Mary could not always help it if her lively imagination – stimulated by her fears – sometimes took over from that point. She usually ended by accusing herself of being no better than the beautiful, jealous creature who had, in her time, so nearly destroyed Nicholas as well as herself.

When she was in that remorseful mood, she leaned over backwards to give Nicholas the reassuring impression that he was as free as air and that she was perfectly happy when he simply had to be away from her. But then a tougher line of approach would suggest itself to her, and she would wonder if she were a fool not to guard her happiness more carefully.

But how? That was the problem. How?

In the end, of course, she told her mother about her engagement. The relationship between her and her parents was too close and frank for her to keep the greatest news of her life to herself.

Her mother was not surprised, she saw. But she did look dubious.

"Well, my dear, I was rather expecting this, of course. If you're sure you can tackle the difficulties there will be –"

"I'm not sure," Mary interrupted with unusually grim candour. "But I love him too much not to try. I had to tell you. He wanted me to, anyway. But perhaps we'd better not tell Dad until the engagement is actually announced."

"Why not?" She saw immediately that her mother resented that. So then she had to explain in detail why the engagement was not being made public for the moment, and it was obvious that her mother regarded the explanation as inadequate.

"Well, I agree it would be better not to tell your father until we can talk about the whole thing openly," she said finally. "He wouldn't like any hole-and-corner arrangement for you, I'm sure."

Mary felt fiercely anxious to defend her glorious, romantic engagement from any such description. But she realised that this was one of the almost unbridgeable gaps between the new life and the old, and that no verbal effort was going to help. To Nicholas it might be perfectly natural to put a veil of secrecy between his private life and his public one. To her mother – and even more to her father – it would merely seem like a lack of candour about something which should be openly and happily discussed.

So she swallowed her resentment and said almost meekly,

"Mother, will you come and meet Nicholas? You could come to the last performance of 'Eugene Onegin' and I'd take you round afterwards."

"Without your father, do you mean?"

"Well, it would have to be, wouldn't it?" Mary explained patiently. "Since we're not telling him for the moment, I mean. And it's next Friday evening, anyway, and Dad's going to be overnight in Northampton, you remember, at that directors' meeting."

"I shouldn't like to do that," Mrs. Barlow stated unequivocally. "I should feel I was being slightly deceitful."

"Oh, Mother, don't be absurd! It's just a question of keeping Dad in the dark a week or two longer because –"

"I've never kept your father in the dark about anything vital."

"But in this particular instance –"

"No, Mary," her mother interrupted firmly, "I know your marriage is going to be a different one from ours. That's as it should be. Every marriage is individual to the people concerned. But I'm telling you here and now, my dear, that *no* marriage is a success where the partners keep each other in the dark about the things which concern them equally."

"But –"

"Let me finish. You are the most vital subject that Dad and I have in common. I'm not going to say I tell him every little worry or thought I have about you, much less what you choose to tell me about yourself. But when it comes to a major decision in connection with you, I'm not going to be one jump ahead of him. When I meet your Nicholas, your father will meet him too. That's the right way for parents to behave, and that's the way I should wish it to be."

When her mother spoke in that tone, Mary knew further argument would be so much wasted breath. And though she felt a certain irritation over her mother's attitude, she could not help envying her the simple, common sense integrity by which she had been able to live her married life.

131

To Nicholas, on their last evening before his departure, she gave a somewhat edited account of her talk. Even then, she was slightly anxious lest he might misunderstand her mother's decision. But she need not have worried. He was absolutely enchanted.

"I love the sound of your mother," he exclaimed. "And as soon as I'm back from this tour I shall meet them both, and everyone will be happy and satisfied."

He was so engagingly sure of this that her own spirits rose – almost to a safe level of comfortable reassurance. This helped her over the hard test of not being able to see him off to Amsterdam, where the first concert was to be. For of course there was no question of her doing any such thing. She was simply the girl in the office, as she had often – and quite sincerely – claimed in earlier days. She had to be satisfied – if that was the word – with a charming photograph in the evening newspapers of Nicholas and Suzanne setting off together at London Airport.

On the first evening he telephoned her. And, brief though the conversation was, it seemed to establish some sort of line with him, and she thought she could get through the next three weeks fairly easily if this were to be the pattern of things.

It was not, however. He was apparently too busy or too much in demand during the evenings to telephone her again. She had a short, affectionate letter. And, apart from that, nothing but the first batch of press cuttings sent by their agent in Holland. These were accompanied by translations, fortunately, and Mary sat in the office devouring them eagerly.

There was no question about the success of the two. One paper said, "It was not a performance, it was an event. An event which one hopes this gifted couple will repeat again and again."

Another one, more chattily, described Suzanne's ravishing appearance, in a dress which had evidently caused a sensation. And all commented on the remarkable way in which the two singers complemented each other's art — "as though they were one", as Mary's least favourite account put it.

It was no wonder that she was looking pale and a little depressed when her employer arrived. And, observant man that he was, he commented on it immediately and asked if she were well.

Mary hastily disclaimed any illness or undue exhaustion. But it seemed that Dermot Deane was not unmindful of devoted service, and that he had his own way of rewarding it.

"I think," he said, sorting through his mail, "that a weekend in Paris would do you good. You can go and have a look at this new lyric who's singing Pamina to Torelli's Queen of the Night. I'd like your opinion of her."

"P-Paris? — Torelli?" gasped Mary. "Do you mean you're sending me over officially?"

"You don't think I expect you to pay your own expenses, do you? You're a good girl, and there are certain perks to this job, you know. It's time your devotion and overtime had some recognition."

"Mr. Deane! I never heard of such a thing! How *good* of you."

"Well, I have my moments," her employer agreed, looking rather pleased with himself. "Here's your air ticket. You leave on Thursday afternoon."

"Thursday —?" Dazedly, she fingered the thin pages of

her air ticket, as though they contained some magic spell. Then she gave a quick gasp. "This says – Amsterdam!"

"Yes. I thought you might like to go by way of Amsterdam, and take in the Brenner-Thomas recital there."

"But it's over!"

"They're doing a repeat. By overwhelming public demand or whatever the term is there."

"And you want me – to go?"

"I thought you would enjoy it," said Dermot Deane, who had claimed that he never interfered in his clients' private affairs. And Mary could willingly have gone across at that moment and kissed him.

"That's why you'll have to leave on Thursday afternoon. I'd be glad if you would look in and handle the morning post first. Then you can catch an afternoon plane and be in good time for the recital in the evening."

"I can't *believe* it!"

"You'll have to fly on to Paris on the Friday morning. The performance there is that evening. Which gives you Saturday and Sunday to yourself in Paris. Now, never say your old employer isn't something of a fairy godfather too!"

"It's the most wonderful – the most terribly generous treat! Terribly expensive –"

"It all goes down against the firm's working expenses," he told her with realistic candour. "Enjoy yourself. Here's where you stay in Amsterdam. Brenner and Suzanne will probably be at the same hotel – we all use it. And this is your address in Paris. Within reason the firm foots the bill. Any wild extravagances you pay for yourself."

"Of course," Mary agreed earnestly. "But there won't be any."

For the rest of that day she had to make a conscious

effort to keep her mind on her work, and away from the wonderful, fairytale trip which was to be hers. In itself it was dazzling enough. But that, in addition, she would be seeing Nicholas in a matter of days! That was almost too wonderful to be believed.

He would be as enchanted as she was. And if Suzanne disliked her sudden arrival, that would be just too bad. She had a perfectly valid reason for being there. The impulse had not been hers. Even the arrangements had not been hers. Dermot Deane had done it all – with what motive Mary was, even now, not quite sure.

She tried that evening to telephone to Nicholas in Cologne, where she reckoned he must now be. But apparently he had left the hotel earlier that day. So she wrote an express letter to the Amsterdam hotel, explaining about Dermot Deane's providential gesture. At last in that way he would know that she was coming, and there would not be the faintest suggestion that she was springing any sort of surprise upon him.

Not that it would be anything but a joyous surprise, of course. But, with the uneasy recollection of Monica perpetually in the background of her mind, Mary was exaggeratedly anxious to avoid the least appearance of keeping a watchful eye on Nicholas.

Somehow she got through the next day or two without any error in her work or major omission in her private life. Once she made something of a gaffe when her mother asked innocently, "Was it really Mr. Deane's own idea that you should go to Amsterdam too?"

"Why, of course, Mother! Who else's?"

"I thought –" her mother smiled – "you might yourself have manufactured a good reason for going to see Nicholas."

"Certainly not! To *spy* on him, do you mean?"

"Don't be so touchy, dear," said her mother mildly. "No one mentioned spying. What a ridiculous word to use!"

It was a ridiculous word. And she was immediately ashamed of having snapped at her mother like that. But she was more than ever glad that she had written so fully to Nicholas, and that he would get the letter before she arrived. He might even be at Amsterdam Airport to meet her! Though on the day of a performance that was by no means certain.

Evidently he had decided against it. Because when her plane touched down, on a perfect late summer afternoon, there was no sign of Nicholas to meet her. The disappointment was small and only momentary. And as she drove into town she was able to enjoy the charming, unfamiliar countryside, and to savour that never-failing thrill of finding oneself abroad in a not too alien country.

At the hotel everything went with the utmost smoothness. Mary signed the register, handed over her luggage and then, on sudden impulse, turned back to the desk. Even though it was the day of the concert, surely she could at least telephone to Nicholas in his room. She asked for his room number.

"Mr. Brenner?" The clerk ran his eye down an alphabetical list. "Mr. Nicholas Brenner?"

"Yes, that's right."

"No, he isn't staying here. He left on the twenty-seventh of last month."

"That was the previous visit. He – they're doing a repeat concert this evening."

"But he is not staying here, madame."

"I sent him a letter –" she tried not to sound as dismayed as she felt. "An express letter."

The clerk obligingly turned to a series of pigeonholes in which mail had been stacked.

"An express letter for Mr. Brenner. Yes, it is here." He produced Mary's own letter for her inspection. "But as he has not been here we could not deliver it."

CHAPTER VII

MARY slowly turned over the letter before returning it to the clerk at the reception desk. Then, as though another thought had just struck her, she asked casually, "And Miss Thomas? Miss Suzanne Thomas. Is she here, by any chance?"

"No, madame. She also left on the twenty-seventh. We have no further reservation for her either."

"Thank you." Mary turned away and followed the small page to the lift.

On the way up to her room she managed to reply smilingly to the boy's comments. She even looked round her room and observed that it was charming – which it was. But, if it had been a dungeon, she could not have felt more chilled and dismayed. And once she was alone she dropped into a chair, without even removing her coat, and tried to assess the significance of the news she had just received.

Nicholas was not here. Nor was Suzanne. There was no question of accommodation not having been available in the hotel generally patronised by Dermot Deane's artists. After all, there had been no difficulty about her own reservation. Quite simply, on their return visit to Amsterdam, Nicholas and Suzanne had gone elsewhere. Together.

"It doesn't mean a thing," Mary told herself without

conviction. "They might be staying with friends. Or one of them might. The other just – just might have preferred a different hotel for some perfectly good reason."

She tried to believe in what she was telling herself. She also tried to recall the commonsense tones of her mother as she had said, "Don't be so touchy, dear. No one mentioned spying. What a ridiculous word to use!"

And yet, sitting here alone in a foreign hotel bedroom, unable to locate Nicholas or prepare him in any way for her coming, she *felt* as though she had been spying. And as though she had just received a nasty and well-deserved shock for her pains.

Only an hour ago there had been nothing but joy in her anticipation of their meeting. Now she began to wonder if it would be wiser not to go to the concert at all. Would Nicholas think that her sudden, unheralded appearance had something a little odd about it?

But the absurdity of being in Amsterdam and not attending the concert for which she had specially come was something she could never explain to her employer. Quite apart from the crushing disappointment she would be inflicting on herself.

Mary put her head in her hands and tried to think what was the natural and sensible thing to do. Suppose she had just been Dermot Deane's secretary, without any personal involvement with either Nicholas or Suzanne, how would she act?

Having checked in at the hotel, enquired after the two artists concerned and discovered that she could not reach them, she would surely give herself up uninhibitedly to the enjoyment of the weekend visit?

There was time for a leisurely and refreshing bath, after which she would change and dine quietly on her own downstairs, and then go to the concert. There would be no question of her disturbing either artist before the performance, but she would of course go backstage afterwards to congratulate them and give them her employer's good wishes.

It seemed a sufficiently sensible and simple programme and, to the best of her ability, Mary followed it out. She had a little difficulty when it came to eating dinner, because she found she had practically no appetite. But she managed reasonably well. Then, having ascertained that the concert hall was only a short distance from the hotel, she set out to walk there through the warm summer evening.

With the surface of her mind she took in the enchanting scene. The evening sunlight on the canals, the boats, the lovely old mellow buildings. She even felt slightly better about her own problems and dared to think that probably, in a matter of hours, everything would be satisfactorily explained and she would be happy and secure again.

The very thought of such relief almost brought tears to her eyes, so that she had to pause a moment and pretend to be gazing with special interest at a magnificent fifteenth-century house on the other side of the canal. As she did so, a vaguely familiar voice just behind her exclaimed,

"It's Dermot Deane's secretary, isn't it? Miss – Miss Barlow. What are you doing here?"

Mary turned quickly, to find herself face to face with Richard Kenning, the accompanist who had gone on the tour with Nicholas and Suzanne, and whom she had met once or twice in the office when the final arrangements were being made.

140

"Hello." She smiled at him. "I'm here for the recital, of course. Mr. Deane, in a madly generous mood, presented me with a long weekend abroad. I'm going to Paris tomorrow, to hear Torelli and this new lyric soprano, and Mr. Deane sent me round by way of Amsterdam so that I could hear the Brenner-Thomas recital too."

"You're in for a treat." Richard Kenning fell into step beside her. "They're in top form, both of them. We've had rave notices everywhere and deserved them. All three of us." He laughed, but evidently, like all really good performers, he knew his own value. "I thought I caught a glimpse of you in the hotel, but then decided I was mistaken. When did you get in?"

"Just a few hours ago. So you're staying at the same hotel?"

"Of course. We most of us use it."

"But Ni- Mr. Brenner and Suzanne aren't there," she said quickly. "I enquired when I arrived."

"No. They're at the Amstel," Kenning informed her carelessly. "They were hatching up something together and thought that was a more impressive setting, I suppose. I happen to prefer something smaller and quieter myself."

She longed to ask outright *what* they had been "hatching up together". But since that would have sounded crude and curious she asked casually instead, "Something professional, do you mean?"

"I expect so. They didn't offer to say, so I didn't ask. With Suzanne particularly it doesn't do to step over whatever line she draws. She has lots of little ploys, both professional and otherwise, that she likes to keep to herself. She's a deep one." He laughed again. "But she certainly is an artist! — Well, I leave you here. Your entrance is round the other side. Enjoy yourself."

He was gone before she could say any more. So she made her way round to the front entrance, wondering whether it would have been cleverer to say, "Don't tell them I'm here," or "Let them know I'm here." As she had not said either, it hardly mattered.

Mary was relieved to find that her seat was halfway back in the hall and rather to the side. That meant she could enjoy the concert – if 'enjoy' were the right word – without much fear of being observed from the platform.

From a purely artistic point of view, it was impossible to do anything but enjoy the concert to the highest degree. Indeed, if Mary had been an uninvolved listener she would probably have rated the occasion among the most beautiful and remarkable she could remember. Both singers were in superb voice and both – which is rare among opera singers – were born recitalists.

Strictly within the framework of the concert platform, they allowed their innate sense of drama to give depth and warmth and colour to their more ambitious numbers. But when it came to the simpler, more unsophisticated songs they both employed a limpid purity of style and tone which, Mary knew, represented highest art.

There were groups of songs where they sang separately, and the flood of pride and love and joy which Mary felt for Nicholas then seemed to wash away all feelings of doubt and unhappiness. But they also sang several duets, and there was no doubt that the artistic sympathy and understanding between them made these the outstanding items in the programme.

Mary was torn between her genuine delight in their shared achievement and her very human dismay at the curious and remarkable oneness which existed between them, at any rate on the platform. Once, when Nicholas took Suzanne's hand and kissed it in tribute to her quite superb performance, Mary felt a sort of constriction round her heart. She recognised it for what it was — an instantaneous and somewhat unworthy sense of jealousy. And she fought it down as she would have fought a personal enemy.

"She *is* wonderful. Why shouldn't he pay tribute to such a colleague before the audience they have both enslaved?" Mary asked herself. And she felt better — as though she had somehow won a small victory — when she was able to clap with as much enthusiasm as anyone else in the audience when Suzanne took a solo bow.

Not until the last group did she begin to feel nervous about going round backstage. The sheer excitement of the concert had held her full attention until that moment. But now — in the next ten or fifteen minutes — she was going to put all her personal anxieties to the test, and all she could think of was how she was going to greet Nicholas. And, still more, how he would take her sudden, unannounced appearance.

Determined not to be involved in the rush backstage that would inevitably follow after the last encore, she slipped out of a side exit as they came on to the platform for the last time. From the passageway she heard Richard Kenning play the opening bars of a provocative, folk-music type of duet with which they had already delighted the audience. Then she went through the pass-door at the end, firmly stating to the man on duty that Mr. Brenner was expecting her and that she was from his London manager.

The not entirely truthful statement took her safely backstage, where the network of corridors was nothing

143

like so complicated as in an opera house. Indeed, when she turned the first corner, she found that she could see straight on to the platform, where Nicholas and Suzanne were laughing and taking their last bows. In turn they bent down to clasp some of the hands which were eagerly held up from the audience. Then, as she saw they were about to leave, Mary instinctively drew back sharply behind her angle of the corridor.

As she did so, she distinctly heard Nicholas exclaim, "Darling, you were superb! I never heard you better in the Rossini."

"Oh, Nick, it's because *you* are there!" Suzanne's lovely husky tones drifted down the corridor. "You *do* something to me. We ought always to be together –"

As Suzanne's voice stopped abruptly Mary was irresistibly impelled to lean forward to see what was happening. And there, framed in the small section of the passage she could see, was Suzanne with her arm round Nicholas's neck, and he was laughing and holding her lightly round the waist as they kissed each other.

Stunned, as though by a physical blow, Mary turned and went out of the building, almost blindly and a little unsteadily, and yet with some sort of instinct which took her unerringly through the nearest exit and into the street. Like someone escaping from a terrible danger, she walked rapidly then, not choosing any direction, not knowing at all where she was going. She just walked – anywhere, so long as it took her away from the scene she had just witnessed.

At first no words formed, even in her mind. Then, when they began to filter into her consciousness, they were not words of her own. They were maddening snatches of what other people had said to her at various times. And all of

144

them seemed to have some horrible bearing on what had happened.

Dermot Deane saying, "This tour will be the test. She's going to mount a pretty powerful campaign, if I'm not much mistaken."

Her mother saying, "There would be a lot of problems in that kind of life —"

Barry, protesting, "It wouldn't be the right life for you. All that stagey glamour, that artificial setting. You are an ordinary girl — in the dearest and most valuable sense of the word."

Barry! who knew her so well, loved her and had offered her security and the kind of life she knew.

And then she remembered Nicholas himself saying, "I thought for a moment you were jealous."

"Oh, Nick, Nick, how could you?" She said the words aloud to the empty street. "You *accused* me of being jealous — made an issue of it. Well, I am jealous, and I have every reason to be. — Oh, where am I? I don't know. And I don't care."

She went on walking, along the bank of one canal and across a bridge and then along the other bank. Sometimes she passed people, singly or in groups. But no one seemed to notice her or find anything unusual about her appearance.

"That's what happens. You're shattered — stunned — almost dead. And the world walks past unknowing. Because your silly little problems are all your own. And no one knows the answer. Not even you, at times."

This time she didn't say the words aloud. She had got past that stage. And presently her pace slackened because she found all at once that she was utterly exhausted, physically and emotionally. The sensible part of her was beginning to realise that she must get back to her hotel. She could not go walking about a foreign city aimlessly and alone at this time of night. But another part of her said it was equally impossible to go back to that hotel bedroom and sit or lie still and think – and think.

In the end, the decision was almost made for her. An unoccupied taxi drew up within yards of her, and by then her weariness was such that she hailed it automatically, muttered the name of her hotel and sank thankfully into its dim obscurity.

Only when she found how long the taxi ride took did she realise how far she must have walked. A sort of dreary somnolence was settling on her by the time they arrived. And, having paid the man, she went into the hotel and to the desk to collect her key in something like a daze.

As she turned away again, her glance idly swept the vestibule and the entrance to the lounge beyond. Then it stopped. For standing in the doorway, with the dimmed lights of the deserted lounge behind him, was Nicholas.

She went slowly forward, but he made no move towards her, nor did he hold out his hands. Only when she came right up to him he said rather hoarsely, "Where, in God's name, have you been?"

"I've been – walking about."

He drew her into the room then, away from the observation of anyone who might come into the hotel. But when he attempted to put his arms round her she pushed him away and said instinctively, "No –"

"Mary, what's the matter? Why are you here in Amsterdam, anyway?"

"I thought –" she gave a cracked little laugh – "you'd be pleased to see me."

"But I *am* pleased to see you! Of course I am. Why

146

didn't you come round after the concert? Kenning said you were in the hall. I couldn't understand —"

"I did come round," she said, slowly and distinctly. "I came round just in time to see you and Suzanne fall into each ohers arms, while you called her 'darling' and she said you ought always to be together."

He went very white. She saw that even in the half-light.

"I did no such —" he began. Then he stopped, as though something knocked faintly at the door of his memory. "It didn't mean a thing!" He spoke almost absently. Then he added, curiously, "Where were you when you heard that, Mary?"

"Near enough to catch every word. I was hidden by an angle in the corridor, but I —"

"You were — hidden by an angle in the corridor," he repeated, and the horror in his expressive voice gave such significance to the words that she exclaimed quickly,

"No — no, it wasn't the way you make it sound. It was —"

"You came from London to Amsterdam, without telling me you were coming —"

"I sent a letter," she cried fruitlessly.

"If Richard hadn't run into you I wouldn't even have known you were here. And you — *hid* in the corridor —"

"I didn't hide! Not deliberately. I didn't want —"

He brushed aside her protest with something like a shudder, and she heard his murmur, "Like a recurring nightmare. Like a nightmare."

"Nick — Nick, please listen to me."

"I'm listening," he said wearily. "I'm listening. But it isn't really necessary. I can tell it to you as well as you can tell it to me. I know it all, like an old record I've heard dozens of times before."

It was she who fell away from him then, the back of her hand pressed against her mouth, in the sudden appalled realisation that nothing she could say would make him believe she had not come jealously to spy upon him. That she was completely innocent, and that she had quite unintentionally stumbled on something for which she might well reproach him, seemed to have nothing to do with the situation now.

To him the point was that he believed she had spied upon him. To her the point was that she felt any jealousy of hers was well merited. They were like people talking different languages. Or like people walking along parallel paths which could never meet.

"It doesn't matter," she said hopelessly at last. "There's nothing either of us could say that would reach the other, in this mood. I'm so tired – and stupid. And you look all in too. We'd be talking in circles."

He made a slight gesture of agreement.

"Tomorrow – perhaps tomorrow –" He turned from her and went slowly towards the door, touching the furniture as he passed, as though he needed some support, or at least the reassurance that there was something concrete in this fog of doubt and wretchedness which had descended upon them.

And she watched him go, without either the heart or the will to tell him that tomorrow she would be gone to Paris, by an early morning plane.

Later, in her room, she thought dazedly, "I let him go. Not just from the hotel, but out of my life. There's no way back after the things we said to each other. I should have tried to justify myself – *now*. Before the certainty of his own belief could be fixed in his mind."

And if she had done so, and he had accepted her faltering explanations in the end — what then? Was it she who had to do the apologising? Was she to accept in her turn that scene between him and Suzanne, with all its implications?

If she had never come to Amsterdam, she would never have known about it. But she *had* come to Amsterdam — and seen for herself. Better to make the break now, before she was more hopelessly involved. At present she could still feel angry with Nicholas, and that gave her a sort of strength.

She stared into the darkness and seemed to see in letters of fire those words of Barry: "It wouldn't be the right life for you."

The next morning she left the hotel early. Even earlier than was necessary in order to catch her plane. But she was suddenly panic-stricken lest Nicholas should come or even telephone before she could get away. And then, when she was sitting in the busy airport, counting off the extra minutes of waiting, the chilling conviction came to her that she had really *hoped* Nicholas would come or telephone.

When she finally heard her flight to Paris announced over the air she had an almost overwhelming desire to turn back. Even now, at this very last half-minute, the decision was still hers. Her luggage would have to go on, of course. But she could follow by another plane. It would take very little while to drive back into Amsterdam. She could go to his hotel. She knew which one it was now.

But then, in imagination, she saw herself walking into the Amstel and asking for Nicholas, and somehow getting Suzanne instead. So she caught her plane to Paris, as arranged. And within an hour or two she was driving down the Champs Elysées for the first time in her life.

149

Bruised and wretched and heartbroken though she was, she could not be entirely indifferent to the most beautiful street in Europe. She gazed around her, faintly comforted by what she saw. And with all her might she tried to wrench her thoughts away from her own miserable little affairs and concentrate on the fact that her employer had trusted her to make some sort of assessment of a new and rising soprano. That meant an evening at the opera which would include, among other things, the supreme experience of hearing Gina Torelli sing the Queen of the Night.

At any other time she would have been excited and thrilled – her first time in the Paris opera, and for such an occasion. But the sombre cast of her spirits kept her calm and serious as she mounted the great staircase of Garnier's beautiful building. And even when the performance began she remained aloof enough to be able to make a well-balanced – though favourable – assessment of the young soprano who was singing Pamina.

But when Torelli made her brief and shattering appearance as the Queen of the Night, Mary sat on the edge of her seat, almost literally, her lips parted in excitement and delight. For, though no longer young, Torelli could still toss off that fiendishly difficult first aria with almost terrifying power and splendour. And the house was hers, as the saying is.

After the performance, Mary went round to see Torelli. Her employer had instructed her to be sure to pay his respects – and hers – to the diva. And, as Mary was no longer so timid about going backstage, she was delighted to have this opportunity of meeting the legendary Torelli at close quarters.

"Dermot sent you?" The great singer surveyed her with

an air of not unfriendly curiosity. "How is he, dear fellow? Still putting on weight?"

Mary replied to this difficult question with what tact she could, and added that she was grateful indeed to her employer for arranging that she should have the tremendous experience of hearing that evening's performance.

"Well –" Torelli smiled indulgently – "it's a favourite role of mine, though it would be unrealistic to pretend that I can go on doing it for many years longer. Which is a pity, because most Queens of the Night are spiritless creatures who only get the role because they can just touch those top notes. She needs to be a demonic force, not a canary in a temper. What did you think of the Pamina?"

"I liked her." Mary felt slightly apprehensive at having to voice her opinion to this forceful lady. "Not a world-shaking voice –"

"Certainly *not*!" interjected Torelli.

"– but I thought she showed great musicality and a real sense of style."

Before she could say more, however, the girl herself tapped on the door and came into the room. She came across and kissed the older woman rather emotionally and then burst into a flood of German, the general gist of which seemed to be that she would never forget Madame's kindness to her.

Torelli replied in equally fluent French, and they appeared to understand each other very satisfactorily, so far as Mary could tell.

But once the girl had gone again Torelli observed, with a shrug, "I didn't understand much of what she said. She talks too fast. But I think it was an elaborate form of saying thank-you. Anyway, she'll do quite well if she works hard."

Mary laughed aloud, and remarked that the soprano seemed a very nice girl, anyway.

"She doesn't need to be a very nice girl," replied Torelli, leaning forward towards the mirror as she added a touch of shadow to her magnificent eyes. "She needs to practise a good legato and keep her diction clear. That's much more important. Her final consonants are sometimes very blurred. Didn't you notice?"

Mary had to admit quite honestly that she had not.

"Well, it takes a good ear to notice these things." Torelli seemed pleased rather than otherwise that Mary had not noticed. "Would you like to come to supper with me?"

"Madame Torelli, I'd *love* to, of course! But why me? There must surely be any number of people who would like to take you to supper."

"Of course. But most of them irritate me. My husband is away on business in the States. I don't usually miss him for a week or two. I hardly notice he's gone," Torelli admitted with candour. "But then I begin to get touchy and restless, and I've reached that stage now. So you had better come with me and amuse me with all the London gossip."

"Willingly. Though I don't think I know much gossip," Mary warned her.

"You must, working in Dermot's office. Did you come straight from London?"

"N-no. I came by way of Amsterdam, so that I could hear the joint recital of Brenner and Suzanne Thomas."

Torelli gave a malicious but extremely musical trill of laughter.

"There, right away, is an item of gossip," she declared. "Is she going to marry the poor Brenner, now that Monica has been rather providentially removed? Come –" she shrugged on a very beautiful mink stole – "we will go somewhere nice and quiet, and you shall tell me all about it."

Nothing was further from Mary's intentions. Though she longed to talk – and hear – about Nicholas, she shrank from the idea of having anything she said subjected to the shrewd scrutiny of Torelli. But the decision was completely out of her hands. Having tackled her stage-door admirers with a sort of brisk graciousness which evidently enchanted them, the diva stepped into her waiting car and, almost before Mary could sit down beside her, said, "Now tell me about Amsterdam."

During the short drive Mary did her best. But her guarded style of describing something that had been so personally wounding to herself hardly satisfied her hostess.

"You make it all sound very dull and uneventful," she said critically. "Was it really like that, or are you perhaps poor at describing things?"

"I think I must be poor at describing things," Mary admitted meekly. "The recital wasn't a bit dull or uneventful. Far from it," she muttered involuntarily as the car stopped outside the restaurant.

Torelli informed her chauffeur that she would not need him again, as she would walk or take a taxi later. Then she swept into the restaurant amid a good deal of fussing and hand-kissing on the part of the gratified proprietor, who evidently knew his famous patron well.

Mary dared to hope that, in the general to-do, the subject of the Amsterdam concert would be dropped. But the hope was vain. Hardly had the waiter departed with their order when Torelli turned to her and enquired, exactly as though there had been no interruption to their conversation,

"What did you mean by that last muttered remark? Why did you say the recital was far from dull and uneventful?"

"I –" Mary, suddenly wordless, looked at her in some dismay.

"Had you some personal stake in it?"

"What makes you think that?" Mary asked rather fearfully.

"The fact that you have a very open face and that I am not exactly a fool," was the brisk reply. Then she sampled the wine which had just been poured out for her to taste, pronounced it unsatisfactory and sent it away.

Mary – who, like most of us, had always wondered if anyone ever really did that – was fascinated. But she remained obstinately silent until the offending bottle had been replaced by one that was approved. Then Torelli said, not unkindly,

"Drink some of your wine. It will make you feel better. I suppose you are yourself in love with Nicholas. He has the misfortune to appeal to almost every type of woman, poor fellow. And you didn't like the possessive way Suzanne swarmed over him. Am I right?"

"So right," replied Mary in a low voice, "that I think you must be something of a witch."

"Most of my rivals would change one letter there," Torelli amended drily. "I'm really neither. But you don't get to the top of my profession by being sweet and silly. Has Nicholas shown any interest in you?"

"Oh, yes. He – he says he loves me."

"He may mean it. Even tenors do sometimes," conceded Torelli. "Why don't you believe him?"

154

"I did, I did! But then, after the recital, I – I came on them in each other's arms, and he was calling her 'darling', and she was saying they ought always to be together –"

Torelli laughed with rather heartless abandon and enquired, as though it really mattered, "Was she hanging round his neck?"

"She was, as a matter of fact," Mary agreed distastefully.

"Yes – yes. The bindweed type," declared Torelli knowledgeably. "Very difficult to detach once they've taken hold. The only defence is quick evasive action beforehand."

"He wasn't taking evasive action," muttered Mary resentfully. "He was calling her 'darling'."

"A very ordinary term of address in our world," Torelli assured her. "Some of us even mean it sometimes. But not often. Now eat your supper, child, and don't take things too much to heart. That scene may not have meant a thing."

Twenty-four hours ago Mary would have argued that passionately. Now, as the good food and wine, and the exhilarating company of Torelli, began to have their affect, she was not so agonisingly certain about the sharp outlines of that scene.

But, if she *had* misinterpreted it, the implications were even more dreadful. It would mean that she had done Nicholas the most horrible and damaging injustice.

"I'll think about it when I'm alone," she told herself desperately. For it was impossible to weigh the pros and cons here and now. Politeness – not to say genuine gratitude – demanded that she gave her full attention to her famous and unexpectedly kind hostess.

When they finally emerged from the restaurant Torelli said, with complete disregard for any wishes but her own, "We will walk a little. My apartment is quite near and I need some air."

So they walked – at an extraordinarily energetic pace. Until Mary, who had already walked miles the previous evening, began to feel she could hardly put one foot in front of the other. Torelli, however, had an unrivalled capacity for not seeing what she did not want to see. She had even, until now, applied this to the Paris traffic. A considerable feat, as everyone will agree.

But, even to the Torellis of this world, there comes a moment when they meet their match. As they turned the last corner before her apartment, and she forged ahead into the road, there was a sharp squeal of brakes too late applied, and for a second Mary thought she was going to see the world's leading soprano swept to her death.

Whether it was professional responsibility, personal attachment, or just sheer instinct Mary never knew. But she instantly stepped out and, catching the singer by the arm, swung her round to safety.

At the same time something hit her very hard. There was a sharp pain in her side and an even sharper pain a second later in her head as she hit the ground. After that she seemed to fall right through the road, down and down and down – into nothing.

CHAPTER VIII

As Mary slowly returned to consciousness once more she realised that she was lying in bed – in a large, soft, elegantly canopied bed, more suited to a stage than anything she had ever occupied before. The room in which she lay was also large, which contributed to the illusion of being in some magnificent stage set, and the sunlight which fell softly through fine net curtains picked out the subdued colours in a carpet of exquisite design.

"I'm dreaming," she decided, and closed her eyes again.

Then she heard a totally unfamiliar voice, with a strong foreign accent, say, "She opened her eyes for a moment, madame. But she is asleep or unconscious again now."

"I'm not asleep," said a weak voice, just above a whisper, and Mary was surprised to realise it was her own.

"Are you not, dear child? Then open your eyes again and try to say a few words to us."

Mary knew *that* voice all right. The strong, beautiful, resonant tones were unmistakable. That was the voice of Gina Torelli, to whom she had been speaking some minutes – or was it hours? – ago.

"I'm all right." She cleared her throat and spoke a little more distinctly. "It was – the taxi, wasn't it?"

"Yes. That taxi!" Torelli used a very naughty and vulgar French expression to describe the taxi-driver who had, broadly speaking, been within his rights when she stepped out in front of him.

Mary opened her eyes again, and this time she was able to focus her gaze on the two women in the room. One of them was a thin, sallow, dark-eyed woman in a white overall. The other was Torelli, clad in a superbly chic black afternoon dress which Mary had never seen before.

"You've changed your dress," she murmured stupidly.

"Changed my dress?" Torelli looked down at herself. "Well, of course, child. I've changed more than once since you last noticed me."

"She must not talk too much, madame," said the other woman.

"Mind your own business, Lisette," snapped Madame.

"It *is* my business to see that she does not tire herself. The doctor said so."

There was mulish obstinacy in the expression of the thin woman and lively annoyance in the face of Torelli. For a moment Mary thought a passionate argument was about to break almost literally over her head. But suddenly, with a self-control which she usually kept only for her singing, Torelli checked herself. Then she said softly, in tones that sounded like a stage benediction, "Sleep a little longer, if you wish to. We will talk later."

So Mary closed her eyes once more, and immediately fell asleep.

When she woke again her mind was much clearer. She knew it must be night-time, or at least late in the evening, for heavy brocade curtains had been drawn across the windows and there was a shaded lamp in one corner of the room, set where the light from it could not disturb her.

Then she thought perhaps it must have been the opening of the door which had roused her. For Torelli came silently across the wide expanse of carpet to stand beside her bed. She was in evening dress, with a long tawny-coloured velvet coat open over her golden dress, and she was wearing the kind of jewellery which made Mary blink.

"You look like Tosca," Mary smiled at her. "You look lovely."

"This light is kind to one," Torelli replied realistically. "And you look much better. How are you feeling now?"

"Nearly all right – I think. Are you going out somewhere?"

"No. I have just come in. I was at a reception at the Elysée. It is after midnight now."

"Which midnight?" asked Mary, making an effort to bring times and days into their proper order. "I mean – how long have I been here in bed?"

"There is no need to worry." Torelli seemed to think she was forestalling some sort of hysterical outburst. "You are getting on very well now. But you were unconscious for more than twenty-four hours."

"Twenty-four hours!"

"Even after that you kept on drifting away again. Sometimes Lisette and I could not leave you at all."

"But, Madame Torelli, have you been nursing me yourself?" Mary was touched beyond expression.

"With Lisette," was the slightly grudging admission. "I suppose Lisette did most of it. But I wished to nurse you too. Why not? You saved my life," she added, dropping her voice a semi-tone or two to express the depth of her feelings.

"Oh, no – not really –" Mary was slightly embarrassed by what she felt to be more than a touch of artistic licence.

"But yes, indeed!" Torelli would not be done out of

her moment of enjoyable drama. "If you had not stepped forward when you did, regardless of yourself – But perhaps it distresses you to recall the scene?"

"Not in the least." Mary shook her head and smiled. "I don't remember much about it. You were almost run down by the taxi, weren't you, and I grabbed you back just in time. But I suppose, as I turned, it hit me. I feel rather –" experimentally she breathed deeply and winced – "my side must have been quite badly bruised."

"You broke a couple of ribs," Torelli informed her. "You are all strapped up. And you were quite badly concussed too."

"But why didn't you have me sent to hospital?" Mary could not help enquiring.

"Hospitals are no good," stated Torelli, who had never been inside one. "A hospital is not the place for someone who has saved my life. I preferred to have you here. Lisette has some experience of nursing, and I also am not a fool. I owed you that at least. I have my faults –" Mary realised this admission was not to be taken too seriously – "but ingratitude is not one of them."

"Thank you. You've been very kind," Mary said. And then, somewhat anxiously as the realities of her position became more clearly defined, she added, "What day of the week is this?"

"Monday."

"Oh, I should have been back in the office this morning! What will Mr. Deane think? – and my mother –"

"It has all been attended to." Torelli calmed her with a kind but authoritative gesture. "I called Dermot last night and explained that you had met with a slight accident and would be staying with me for the rest of the week. He undertook to inform your family. In a day or two I shall

160

telephone again, to say you will stay longer. In this way no one will be excessively anxious. And by the time we have to admit you have been rather ill the worst will be over."

"I don't think that will satisfy my mother! She would much rather know the truth, I'm sure. I think I should phone her, if you don't mind."

"Not tonight, dear. Tomorrow you shall."

Mary remembered then that it was after midnight, and any telephone call at that time of night would increase rather than quiet her mother's anxieties.

"First thing in the morning then – please," she begged. And to this Torelli agreed.

She had a rather restless night after that. During the hours of sleep or unconsciousness her worries and problems had been suspended. But, now that her mind was active again, her thoughts ranged backwards and forwards, not only over her mother's possible anxieties and the inconvenience to her employer, but over the events immediately preceding her journey to Paris.

What had Nicholas thought when he found her gone? They had parted on such a confused and discordant note that, at the time, the break had seemed to her final and inevitable. In her dismayed certainty that he had been betraying her with Suzanne she *intended* that break to be final. It had seemed to her the only answer.

But since then something of Torelli's trenchant good sense had been poured over her. And in one layer of her consciousness some of that lingered, to colour her own more reasonable second thoughts.

Was it possible, she wondered now, that, in her insecurity and loneliness – and jealousy, for she must not make excuses for herself – she had given the most absurd significance to a scene which could be duplicated over and over again between stage colleagues sharing a moment of excited triumph?

Nicholas himself had said, "It didn't mean a thing." And Torelli, speaking with careless, scornful confidence at the supper table, had used exactly the same expression: "That scene might not have meant a thing."

Only to Mary, insecure, unknowing and scared, it had meant so much – so much. And because of it, on impulse, she had rushed away into the night, her anger hot and her judgment clouded.

By the time she came face to face with Nicholas she was in a fever of doubt and misery and all she could do was pour out her furious, agonised suspicions. But how, she wondered now, must that have appeared to *him*?

Unannounced and without warning, she had erupted into his professional world. Not the quiet girl with the beautifully pitched voice which soothed his tense nerves, but someone who seemed to have been following him round, trying in some vulgar way to see what he was up to when she was not there.

Mary gave a little groan which had nothing to do with the dull ache in her cracked ribs. It was because, slowly but irresistibly, she was recalling that scene as he must have viewed it. She could not remember her exact words. She only knew that she must have seemed like the terrible echo of the unhappy Monica, who had poisoned both their lives with just such unreasonable jealous outbursts.

"Oh, I didn't mean it! Nicholas, I didn't mean it," she whispered into the darkness. And as she did so, she found herself wondering if perhaps Monica had not meant it either in the beginning. – If perhaps she had just let the

162

cancer of her jealousy grow upon her until it almost destroyed them both.

"If I can have another chance! Oh, *please*, if I can have another chance." That was Mary's last thought as she fell asleep again.

The next morning, Torelli was as good as her word. A telephone was brought to Mary and plugged in beside the bed by Lisette, who informed her that she was to talk to her mother for as long as she liked.

It was a wonderfully healing and reassuring conversation. After all she had been through, Mary felt she had never before so valued her mother's kindly composure and common sense. Yes, they had been anxious, of course, though a good deal reassured to hear that she was being looked after by the famous Gina Torelli. And how was dear Mary feeling now?

Dear Mary was able to reassure her mother that she was rapidly improving. She owned to the cracked ribs and the concussion, though she refrained from saying just how long she had been unconscious.

"But why aren't you in hospital, you poor child?" her mother not unnaturally demanded. And Mary had to explain about Torelli not believing in hospitals (to which her mother said, "What nonsense!") and how the singer had some exaggerated idea that Mary had saved her life and therefore insisted on looking after her in her own home.

"Well, so long as you're being *properly* looked after —" Mrs. Barlow said doubtfully.

"Oh, Mother, of course I am! You have no idea what care and luxury are being lavished on me."

"And you don't feel that your father or I should come over?"

"No, truly not. I expect I'll be allowed to travel in a

few days. Well — a week, anyway."

So her mother was more or less satisfied, and Mary was free to stay where she was and enjoy the sensation of feeling a little stronger each day. She was pampered beyond belief. She could hardly express a wish without having it granted, and every delicacy of French cooking was there to tempt her naturally very healthy appetite.

Torelli brought her papers and magazines, in a variety of languages, for her amusement and edification. And it was in one of these that she came across a photograph of Nicholas. A full-page photograph of him smiling, with a caption about one of his German appearances. On the facing page, inevitably, there was a photograph of Suzanne, but by turning back the page Mary could avoid looking at that. Instead, she lay there gazing at the strong yet sensitive face of the man she loved.

For so long now, it seemed to her, she had recalled him only in a tragic mood. But now, as she looked into those smiling eyes, she could see him once more in the gay early days of their acquaintanceship, when everything had seemed to go well. They had laughed a good deal together then, she recalled, with surprise and indescribable nostalgia. She had seemed to know how to charm away those occasional moments of remembered tragedy, and he had looked at her as though he saw the sun come out from behind clouds. Those were the happy days when he had been sure of her trust and understanding, and the nightmare of his past life with Monica had almost left him.

"Oh, my dear!" she actually addressed the photograph. "Give me just one more chance, and I'll never, never, never let you down again."

She was still gazing at him when Torelli came into the room. And, although she hastily tried to turn the page, the singer's keen powers of observation were quicker.

"Aha, you've found the charming photograph, I see." Torelli picked up the magazine in her strong, capable hands. "He really is an attractive brute. Almost too much so." She studied the page. "There's something beguiling about a tenor voice that already gives them an unfair advantage. The good looks ought to go to the baritones and basses if life were strictly fair, which of course it isn't."

Before Mary had time to consider this interesting theory, Lisette followed her mistress into the room, holding some letters in her hand.

"The post has come, Madame. You wanted —"

"Oh, to be sure!" Torelli took the letters and quickly shuffled through them until she found the one she evidently wanted. "From my husband," she explained to Mary in parenthesis. "And about time too!" she added, with a curious note of almost bullying affection in her expressive voice which secretly amused and intrigued Mary.

Torelli turned away, presumably to go and enjoy her letter on her own. But at the door she paused, glanced down at a larger envelope among those in her hand and observed, "From Dermot, I see. And with an enclosure. I suppose it might be —" She slit open the envelope with one of those strong, decisive movements so characteristic of her.

"Yes — here you are." She came back to the bed with a thin, foreign-looking letter in her hand, which she examined with frank interest, curiosity being a perfectly permissible emotion in her opinion. At least, so far as she herself was concerned. "From Amsterdam. Now I *know* that writing. Handwriting always interests me. So revealing."

She continued to look at the letter for a moment, while Mary could scarcely restrain the impulse to snatch it from her.

"Why, of course! It's Nick Brenner's writing. And about time *he* wrote too! These men! Who do they think they are?" And she good-naturedly tossed the letter on to the bed and went out of the room, leaving Mary shaking with mingled hope and fear.

But hope was uppermost. For her own change of heart about the last scene with Nicholas was so complete – her good intentions for the future so clear – that it seemed impossible that he might not feel as she did.

She drew the one sheet of paper from the envelope and, even at a glance, she thought that the handwriting, with its heavily accented downstrokes, bespoke agitation, as though the writer had driven his pen hard into the paper with the intensity of his feelings.

"Mary –" he had written, without any "dear" or "darling" to soften it – "What can I say to you – what can either of us say to each other – after last night? The scene must have been as horribly revealing to you as to me. For a few short, wonderful weeks I had thought that there was not only love but complete trust and understanding between us. Now I see that such a thing doesn't exist. Perhaps it doesn't exist between any man and woman in the sense I mean. I don't know. Possibly it's I who am unreasonable, and you who are the norm. If so, I accept the responsibility of this disaster as mine. I expected too much and was unfair to do so. But if that is how it has to be then marriage – any marriage – is not for me.

"I'm trying not to blame you unduly. God knows, I can't afford to criticise others, with one marriage failure already behind me. But surely somewhere there must be someone who means the same as I do by the words 'trust' and 'understanding'. When I realised you had been spying on me, very much as Monica used to spy on me, I knew it was the end. Yet I had to see you, to seek some explanation – any explanation. And all you had to offer me were the hideously familiar reproaches and suspicions.

"I'm not questioning your love, Mary. But I just can't live with a stifling, demanding, jealous love like that. I wish I could see some future for us – but I know there is none. You probably know it too in your heart.

" 'Addio' is the saddest word in the Italian language. Perhaps that is why Puccini's Mimi softened it magically with the words 'senza rancor' – without ill-feeling. I'm sorry, my dear, but that's what it has come to with us. Addio, senza rancor – Nicholas."

"I don't believe it." Mary realised that she had actually whispered the words aloud. "I don't believe it."

But she had to believe it. He had written it all down, exactly as it must have seemed to him. And he had ended with an absolutely final farewell.

She made herself read it again – every wounding word of it – and she felt overwhelmed by remorse and a sense of her own inadequacy. For she had failed him. That was the sum total of it. She had failed him. She loved him – how she loved him! – she had wanted to support and sustain him, and she had thought she understood him. But when it came to the crunch – she had failed him.

If he had come into the room at that moment and stood before her, there was nothing she could think of that she would have been able to say to him in extenuation of her behaviour. Just perhaps the small, small fact that she had written to him first to tell him she was coming to Amsterdam. At least she had not crept up on him unawares, as he

167

believed. But that seemed small now, measured against what had followed.

For a long time she lay there, holding back her tears and swallowing the lump that kept on coming into her throat. She was still doing that when Lisette came in with her lunch and, tempting though it looked, Mary said immediately that she didn't want anything to eat.

"Of course you do. It is lunchtime and you must eat." Lisette spoke as though she were dealing with a fractious child.

"I'm not hungry." Mary turned her head away.

"Are you not well again?"

"I'm just not hungry. I don't want any lunch."

Lisette, who was used of course to every sort and kind of temperamental reaction, muttered to herself in French and went out of the room again. Three minutes later Torelli entered.

"What is this nonsense about no lunch?" Torelli's methods were even more direct than Lisette's.

"Just that. I'm not hungry."

"It is not necessary to be hungry. But you must eat, otherwise you will not get well. And then when you die of malnutrition your mother will blame me."

Mary wanted to say that her mother would never do anything so illogical. But instead she began to cry.

For a moment Torelli regarded her consideringly. Then her glance fell on the letter still open on the bed, and she picked it up.

"I suppose that stupid Russian is responsible," she said, ruthlessly stripping Nicholas of his half-British nationality in this moment of censure. "May I read this?"

Mary made an instinctive gesture of dissent. Then,

feeling that nothing in the world mattered much now, she nodded.

With some deliberation Torelli proceeded to read. Mary kept her head turned away for most of the time. But finally she could not resist glancing at Torelli to see the effect of Nicholas's words upon her.

"It's a nice touch at the end," Torelli observed approvingly. " '*Addio, senza rancor!*' There's the real artist." And she actually sang the famous phrase, in half-tone but so beautifully that Mary immediately felt the tears come into her eyes again. "Did you really behave in this silly way?" Torelli wanted to know.

"It – it wasn't quite as he thought," Mary murmured in self-defence.

"It never is when two people who are in love fall out." replied Torelli with rather touching truth. "Cheer up, dear child. There will almost certainly be a chance to explain and apologise."

"How can there be?" Mary demanded forlornly. "With him in one country and me in another, and neither of us in the right one, come to that."

"There is no such thing as the *right* country," Torelli told her severely. "All have their particular advantages. That is why I, for instance, pretend to be Italian, prefer to live in France, and hold on to my British nationality like grim death. You must not allow yourself to become narrow-minded just because you happen to be disillusioned for the moment."

This totally irrelevant and rather unfair attack served to distract Mary's attention from her misery for a moment. And Torelli went on, "Once you are able to get about again everything will seem different. Meanwhile, he at least is mobile. He may well come rushing to Paris to see you when he hears that you are ill."

"After that letter? How could he?" Mary rejected the idea almost fretfully. "No man would do such a thing."

"On the contrary, many of them would. Men are constantly doing the most idiotic things," Torelli asserted. "They *are* idiotic, by and large. Women too, of course," she added with strict impartiality. "But in a different way. Now will you eat your lunch?"

There seemed nothing else for it. So Lisette brought back her lunch and Mary contrived to eat it, with a faint return of her normal appetite. For one thing, completely illogical though Torelli's arguments might·be, they had been advanced with such confidence, and with such an air of knowing all about the mad world of the artist, that there was an odd sort of comfort about them.

For most of that afternoon Mary lay there, alternating between the depths of her natural despair and the somewhat unrealistic optimism generated by Torelli's bracing assertions. Was it possible? Could she – *dared* she – believe that when Nicholas heard of her accident he might still care enough to be anxious and feel impelled to come to Paris for himself and find out how badly she had been injured?

The idea was so deliciously comforting that she allowed her thoughts to play around it, until she almost convinced herself that it was the logical conclusion to all that had happened.

She could actually imagine the details of his arrival – the sound of his footsteps in the hall, the opening of the door. It was difficult to think just what she would say to him. But perhaps there would be no need to say anything. Pale with anxiety and the intensity of his feelings, he would just come straight across the room and take her in his arms, and somehow the explanations would take care of themselves.

At this point she realised that she was half asleep and that practical possibilities had slipped into wishful day-dreaming. So she roused herself and read his letter again, and was instantly plunged into fresh despair.

The chill of the written word is always more final than anything actually spoken, and now she could not imagine why she had not had the courage and sense to stay and talk things out with him. She could have made *some* sort of defence, however much she might have been in the wrong. Instead of which, she had left him to commit his thoughts and fears to paper, which must inevitably have impressed them even more powerfully on his own mind.

At that point her spirits slipped to their very lowest ebb. Then the blackness of her despair was pierced by the entry of Lisette with a slight air of mystery about her. And what she said was,

"Do you feel well enough to have a visitor?"

"A visitor, Lisette?" Suddenly she rocketed to such dizzy heights of hope that she actually caught her breath. "Yes, of course! Who is it?"

"A very good-looking young man," replied Lisette, with an unexpected dash of coquetry which sat oddly upon her. "He just said to tell you he thought you would be glad to see him."

Glad to see him! Nothing – nothing in the whole world – could express her gladness. The heavens opened and the angels sang. And dear, dear clever Torelli had been right. He had come!

Mary sat up, pushed back her hair and reached for the

171

very becoming dressing-jacket which was a present from Torelli.

"Do I look all right, Lisette?"

"I guess he'll think so," Lisette laughed. "Shall I show him in?"

"Yes, please!"

She heard his step in the hall, just as she had imagined. She heard it even above the loud beating of her own heart, and she *willed* him to come straight across and take her in his arms.

The door swung open, propelled by Lisette's willing hand. And suddenly Mary's heart gave a sickening downward lurch.

For it was not Nicholas who came into the room with an eager, anxious smile. It was Barry.

CHAPTER IX

"Oh, Barry – dear! How good of you to come."

Somehow she managed to get out the appropriately grateful words, to smile at him with an appearance of delighted surprise, to hold up her face for his anxious, affectionate kiss, to hide the bitter disappointment that he was Barry and not Nicholas.

Fortunately, he seemed to find it quite natural that he should do all the talking at first. That gave her time to collect her thoughts and to realise that, if she had not been indulging in absurd day-dreams about Nicholas, she would have been happy indeed to see Barry, or anyone else from home.

"What brought you here? What a lovely surprise!" She could say that now with some sincerity.

"I phoned yesterday evening to ask you to come to a show, and your mother told me about your accident. I couldn't rest until I had come to see for myself how you really were."

"That was kind of you, Barry." And she thought, "Mother would be well impressed by that. She's probably thinking more approvingly of him now than she ever did before."

"Nothing kind about it," he insisted. "I just had to know. How are you feeling now, darling?"

He looked at her so tenderly that it would have been churlish to query, even mentally, his right to call her "darling". So she let him continue to hold the hand he had taken, while she gave him a favourable account of her progress.

At the conclusion of this he immediately began to talk of the possibilities of getting her home, and she found herself listening eagerly. Until then she had been content to exist in a sort of luxurious vacuum. Now, as he spoke of the dear, familiar, everyday details of home, she realised that she longed passionately to be there.

"Nothing could be simpler," he assured her. "Once you're allowed up and have gathered some strength together, you could be driven to the airport, taken to the plane in a wheeled chair and flown to London Airport where I could meet you."

"I'm already being allowed up for a little while each day," she told him.

"Well, there you are! It's probably only a question of a day or two before we can have you home."

"Do you really think so?" Her eyes sparkled. "Not that I haven't been very happy here," she added quickly. "Madame Torelli has been incredibly kind. And I think she rather enjoyed having me. I was a bit like a new toy to her."

"Good lord!" said Barry. "What an extraordinary idea."

"Oh, no, not really. She dramatises everything, and liked to think I had saved her life, just because I pulled her out of the way of a taxi and got bumped myself. She's a trifle bored when her husband is away and I filled the gap. But he's due back at the end of the week and, from something Lisette said, I believe they had planned to go

174

to the South of France. I daresay it would suit them both very well if I were well enough to go home soon."

This was not quite what Torelli admitted to when she came in. For one thing, she preferred to make any arrangements herself and was not too pleased with Barry for taking the initiative. But he exerted all the charm and persuasion which had helped to put him at the top of his firm, and presently she did concede that, provided it could be arranged with no harm to Mary, her return home would indeed fit in with the plans she and her husband had in mind.

Barry had to return to London that same evening, so his visit was necessarily brief. But before he left a great deal had been arranged. The doctor's permission for Mary to travel had been sought and obtained, the air reservation confirmed, and arrangements made for her to have an invalid's treatment on the flight.

Once he had gone, Torelli asked with customary curiosity, "And where does *he* come in?"

"Barry? I suppose you could describe him as an old flame of mine," Mary said lightly. "I was very sweet on him once, then he nearly married another girl. But that didn't come off, and he and I became friends again."

"Friends?" Torelli rejected the word with splendid scorn. "The man's in love with you."

Mary was silent. And after a pause Torelli said consideringly, "He might be a lot better for you than Nicholas Brenner. More your type – conventional without being dull. Rather charming. And he'd wear well." She paused again and then added on a note of not unkindly warning, "We artists are difficult to live with, you know."

"I know," said Mary.

"Well –" Torelli slightly raised her expressive hands

and let them fall again – "I won't say any more. People don't really ever want to hear advice, however good it may be."

"That's what my mother says," Mary smiled. "She says people only want someone to tell them what they want to hear."

"I think," said Torelli, "that I should like your mother."

"I'm pretty sure," replied Mary with some surprise, "that she would like you. You couldn't be more different in most ways. But you both have the same sort of basic common sense."

"Ah – common sense!" The singer gave her quite lovely smile. "A most precious commodity, and almost always in short supply, as the ridiculous modern phrase has it." Then she added, with apparent irrelevance, "I was talking to Dermot on the phone earlier today. He wants me to come to London for a concert towards the end of the year."

"Oh, do! Please, please come. It would be wonderful. I've never heard you in a concert."

"I'm good," stated Torelli without false modesty.

"If you'll come and do the concert I'll promise not to burst into tears when I have to say good-bye. Much though I shall want to."

"Emotional blackmail," observed Torelli, looking extremely pleased. "All right, you can tell Dermot I agree. But with a ten per cent increase on my previous fee. Costs are rising every day. And now – no tears, mind. I dislike tears except as a tribute to one of my operatic performances."

So even when it came to saying good-bye some days later, Mary gallantly controlled her emotions, although she did cling to Torelli and kiss her with some fervour.

"There, there." Torelli patted her shoulder brusquely. "Come and see me when you're next in Paris." She spoke as though Mary might make a habit of whisking across the Channel whenever the mood took her. "Let me know if they don't treat you properly on the journey and I'll give the airline hell. I know one of the directors."

There was no need, however, to have this threat implemented. Mary was looked after like precious china all the way, and was eventually handed over to Barry at London Airport by an attractive air hostess.

She was tired by then, in spite of all the comfort and care, and was glad just to sit back in the car beside Barry, with the pleasant awareness that she was on the last lap home.

He glanced at her anxiously once and said, "You're all right, aren't you? I didn't hustle you back too soon."

"No, no, I'm quite all right so long as I make no sort of effort. It's lovely just to sit here knowing you'll look after everything and get me home safely."

"Of course, my darling. That's what I'm here for."

She wanted to tell him that alas, she was not his darling. Not now nor at any other time. She valued his friendship and was infinitely grateful for the way he looked after her. But when it came to being someone's darling, if she could not be Nicholas's darling she was no one's. Sometime she would have to convince Barry of this. But today was hardly the day to tell him.

At home once more, in her mother's care, Mary felt a different being. The luxurious indulgence of the Torelli ménage might be missing, but all the familiar affection and security lapped her round, and she throve like a plant in its natural soil. Indeed, within a matter of days, she was already talking of going back to the office, even if for only

177

a few hours a day.

"Barry won't approve," remarked her mother. "He's still phoning daily to ask how you are."

"Barry? It has nothing to do with Barry," Mary said quickly. Then, as her mother looked thoughtful, she added rather awkwardly, "I appreciate all he's done, Mother, and I'm glad you've seen his better side now. But — but don't *encourage* him in any way, will you?"

"It isn't my encouragement he wants." Her mother looked amused. "The question is — do *you* want to encourage him?"

"No," said Mary, without elaboration.

"Then it's still Nicholas Brenner?" her mother said after a pause. And Mary nodded rather unhappily.

Characteristically, her mother did not press her further. But later, when she was alone in her own room, Mary opened a drawer and took out the magnificent ring which Nicholas had given her.

It was not really hers any longer, of course. When an engagement was broken the right thing to do was to return the ring. And yet to send back his ring, as the only answer to his letter, was to accept the justice of what he had written and quench the last glimmer of hope.

That she had any hope left at all both surprised and slightly shamed her. But almost defiantly she picked up the ring and slid it on to her finger, and immediately her hand clenched round it in a little spasm of anguish, as though every natural instinct resisted the idea, however logical, that she must part with this one symbol of the fact that Nicholas had once loved her.

It would not be possible to wear the ring openly, of course. It never had been possible, she reflected sadly. But if she could find a chain —

Suddenly she began to rummage through her modest jewel box, until she found a slender gold chain which had once belonged to her grandmother, and on this she threaded Nicholas's ring, and hung it round her neck. Cool and hard, it slid down inside her dress, and oddly enough, she found some sort of comfort in the feel of it.

After that the only thing she could think of was to get back to the office. Surely there she would catch some breath of news of him. Dermot Deane must know where — or if — he was in the country, and something of what he was doing.

When she announced her intention of returning to work her father made a few anxious objections. But her mother simply said, "Let the child decide for herself. She knows her own strength best. But perhaps you'd better drive her down. She shouldn't be struggling on and off trains in the rush-hour yet."

So Mary was taken by car to the office, where her reception both touched and surprised her. Her employer actually kissed her and declared he had been lost without her. And although she knew he had managed very well for something like thirty years before she had even come on the scene, she found this piece of exaggeration very heart-warming.

He wanted to know the details of her stay with Torelli and remarked, "You seem to have made a real hit with her. I gather it's thanks to you that she's accepted the London concert."

"Nothing of the sort," Mary assured him. "That's a little bit of play-acting on her part. She likes the idea that she was snatched from death by a devoted admirer whereas, in actual fact — and between these four walls — she richly deserved to have been run over, and I only happened to be the handy person who yanked her back in time. But she's a darling and I adore her, and I quite understand why everyone puts up with her nonsense, because at heart she's real and warm — and oh, what an artist!"

"I agree with every word of that," Dermot Deane grinned indulgently. "I even agree to the demand for the extra ten per cent. Why not? She's worth six of the dimly twinkling little starlets today. But that also is between these four walls. How did you get on in Amsterdam?"

"It was a superb occasion." Mary simply willed her heart not to beat any faster. "Are they both back in England?"

"Came back a week ago. Suzanne came in to see me before going back to Canada. I don't know about Brenner. I haven't seen him."

"Wasn't it more or less settled that he should stay in this country quite a while, to study Marcus Bannister's new work with him?" she managed to ask coolly.

"That was the long-term plan — yes. But you never know with these artists. They chop and change a lot. He'll be dropping in one of these days, no doubt, if only to collect his mail."

And with that Mary had to be satisfied, and somehow keep herself from actually biting her nails with impatience and frustration.

She was not allowed to work at all hard during that first day, and halfway through the afternoon her employer was just proposing to send her home when Anthea Warrender came in, on her way to a late rehearsal. She was openly pleased to see Mary, and enquired about her welfare so kindly that it was suddenly quite easy to ask,

"Have you seen anything of Ni- of Mr. Brenner since

he came back from the continent?"

"I was just going to ask *you* that," Anthea countered. "Have you run into him?"

"No," Mary said, unaware how forlorn that sounded. "No, I haven't."

There was silence for a moment. Then Dermot Deane said she had better go now if she wanted to avoid the rush-hour.

"Yes, you don't look as though you could do much battling yet," Anthea remarked. And then, as though a pleasing idea had struck her, she added, "Why don't you come down to us for next weekend? It's lovely by the river just now, and I'd make it my business to spoil you at least as well as Torelli."

"How kind of you!" Mary thought of the beautiful house where she had first began to hope that Nicholas loved her, but which was now full of poignant memories. "I would willingly, but my mother's rather enjoying having me under her eye for the moment, and I think she'd be disappointed if I left just now."

"I understand. My mother would be the same," Anthea agreed unexpectedly. "Another time, then." And she dropped a light kiss on Dermot's balding head, waved to Mary and went off.

"That's a lovely girl," remarked Mary's employer. "Too good for Warrender."

"But he adores her!" protested Mary.

"Oh, yes, in his demanding, dictatorial way. Very wearing sometimes, I should think. Would *you* like to be adored by Oscar Warrender?"

"Certainly not!" said Mary, who wanted to be adored by Nicholas Brenner and no one else at all.

"Well, there you are, then." Dermot smiled at her, but

his glance was shrewd. "You're looking a bit pale and peaky by now. Today was a good effort, and I appreciate your making it. But take it easy tomorrow. There's no need to come in. It will be a slack day and I shan't need you."

"You're quite sure?" The suggestion was more welcome than she wanted to admit, for she felt unexpectedly tired by now.

"Quite sure. Go along with you."

So Mary went, and was glad enough to go straight to bed when she reached home.

"If I feel stronger again in the morning I shall go," she told her mother. But when it came to the point she was relieved not to have to repeat the previous day's effort.

The following day, however, she woke feeling entirely different and she realised that she had come to that turning point which marks almost all periods of convalescence when suddenly one is something like one's real self again. She yielded to her father's insistence on giving her a lift once more, but she knew it was hardly necessary. And when she walked into the office it was with such a brisk step and such an eager air that her employer exclaimed,

"Ah, that's my girl again! You look quite different."

"I feel quite different," Mary told him. "I'm really ready for work again, though I was glad of the rest yesterday. How did things go?"

"You mean – how did I possibly manage without you?"

"I didn't mean that at all! I meant – was it as slack as you expected?"

"Pretty well. By the way, your favourite came in."

"My favourite?" She turned sharply from hanging up her coat. "Who do you mean?"

"Brenner, of course. He's your favourite, isn't he?"

She didn't answer that. She couldn't answer at all for a moment. She was struggling too hard to hide her bitter disappointment at having missed him.

"He seemed very shocked about your accident," her employer went on. "He heard about it only recently — from Anthea, I believe."

"What did he say? about me — about my accident, I mean."

"Just that. That he was shocked, and he wanted to know how you were. Nothing else much. He didn't stay long. Only came in to collect his mail, and there was little enough of that, as it happened. Just a letter sent on from the Amsterdam hotel."

"The Amsterdam hotel?" There must have been an odd note in her voice because Dermot Deane glanced enquiringly at her. "What — what did he do with it?"

"*Do* with it? What does one do with out-of-date fan mail? Chucked it in the wastepaper basket, I suppose."

"He did that? You saw him do that?"

"No." Her employer was looking extremely surprised by now. "He shoved it in his pocket, if I remember rightly, and threw it in the wastepaper basket when he got home, I imagine. Does it matter?"

"No," said Mary, uttering this thumping lie with desperate calm. "It doesn't matter really. It's just that I always have a certain sympathy for fans, having been one myself."

Dermot Deane laughed callously at that, declaring that experience would teach her to be less soft-hearted. And so she had to manage to smile and go to her desk and get on with the morning's work.

It was all she could do to keep her attention on what she

was doing, for hammering insistently at the back of her mind, were half a dozen anxious questions.

Had Nicholas destroyed her letter unread? To the best of her remembrance, he had never had occasion to see her handwriting, so why should he connect her in any way with the readdressed envelope? And then if – kinder than Dermot – he did open the letter and glance at the signature, was his anger and disillusionment such that he would just crumple it up and throw it away?

To that question she felt the answer must be "No". Nicholas was neither petty nor ill-tempered – and surely sheer curiosity would make him turn to the beginning again and read? Would the date convey to him immediately the importance of that mislaid letter? Had she even *put* a date, now she came to think of it?

And, when she had exhausted all the possibilities and improbabilities connected with the letter, came the most chilling question of all. Was it quite possibly not her letter at all? He might well have had hers long ago and found nothing in it to modify his fixed opinion that all was over between them. In which case, this was no more than her employer thought it was – an out-of-date piece of fan mail.

"That's it," she told herself. "You're getting excited about something utterly unimportant." But then back would come the questions, clamouring for an answer.

Not long after lunch Anthea came in again, looking unusually harassed for her.

"Dermot, I'm in a jam!" She flung out her hands expressively. "Can I borrow Mary? If she's willing, I mean."

"I expect so." Dermot smiled indulgently. "For how long and for what purpose?"

"For the afternoon. And to fetch my score from home. I've stupidly left it there, and it's an important rehearsal today."

"We have most of the standard scores here." Dermot gestured towards one of the big office cupboards. "What do you want?"

"No, no, you don't understand. It has to be my own copy. The one Oscar marked for me with everything just as he wants it. He'll be furious if I haven't got it on this day of all days."

"Let him be furious. Do him good," Dermot began.

But Mary interrupted to say, "Of course I'll go! How do I get there? I was taken by car last time, you remember."

"Yes, of course. You're an angel, Mary. If you take a taxi to Paddington right away you'll just catch the five past three. It doesn't take more than half an hour, and I'll phone Trudi to see there's a car waiting for you at the station. She'll know where to find the score too, when you get to the house."

"Why not get her to send the score with the car?" suggested Dermot practically.

"Oh, Dermot!" Anthea turned on him with the only spurt of temper Mary had ever seen her display. "Will you stop *interfering*? I know what I'm doing. Trudi may have to look for the thing."

"Sorry, sorry. Don't mind me." Dermot put a hand in mock self-defence. And suddenly Anthea gave him a remorseful smile and said,

"No – *I'm* sorry. I was being temperamental, wasn't I?"

"Just a bit. But it suits you. And it's nice to know Oscar isn't the only one in the Warrender family to ride high.

185

— Off you go, Mary."

So Mary went. And, in the taxi on the way to Paddington, she realised how disappointed she would have been if she had been deprived of this chance to catch a glimpse once more of the house where so much had happened to her and Nicholas.

She caught her train with five minutes to spare, and at the other end of her journey there was a car waiting for her. The drive was longer than she had expected, but it was a beautiful afternoon, and she looked out on the late autumnal scene with that touch of enjoyable melancholy which most of us associate with that season.

It had been the high summer of her hopes when she had come before. But she refused to allow too many regrets to shadow this unexpected journey back into the lovely past. If she spent only a few minutes in the house she intended to enjoy them.

It seemed, however, that she was to spend more than a few minutes there. Trudi – the Warrenders' very efficient maid – met her at the door with many apologies. Madame, it seemed, had telephoned with the utmost regret for her stupidity. She had found the score in her dressing-room, after all, and she begged Mary to forgive her for having sent her on a totally unnecessary journey.

"It doesn't matter a bit," Mary assured the apologetic Trudi. "We all do these things. And Mrs. Warrender had a lot on her mind with this important rehearsal. I quite enjoyed the break from office routine anyway." She laughed. "And I – I like seeing the house again." She glanced round appreciatively.

"Madame said I was to be sure to give you tea," Trudi explained. And, when Mary protested this was quite unnecessary, she said earnestly, "Please, Miss Barlow. She would be very upset if I let you go back without tea. If you will go through into the studio, I will bring it there. You remember the way, don't you?"

Yes, she remembered the way. The way to the long, lovely room where Nicholas had sung to her that compelling love song of Marcus Bannister's.

With her heart full of memories, Mary crossed the hall to the studio. And as she entered the room Nicholas got up hastily, almost agitatedly, from a chair by the window.

"Nicholas!" She stood stock still gazing at him, her hand against her cheek.

"What are you doing here?" Agitation lent a faintly harsh note to his usually musical voice. "Why have you come?"

"I wouldn't have come if I'd known you were here!" She spoke in quick self-defence, *her* tone sounding almost aggressive in her anxiety to explain away her presence. "Anthea thought she had forgotten her score, and I came to fetch it. But she hadn't forgotten it after all." The explanation poured out jerkily.

"You mean it was an invented excuse to get you down here?"

"If so, the invention was hers, not mine!" Mary felt the angry colour flare in her cheeks. "There was no need for me to see you – after that letter. No need at all." Then, as the lengthening silence cried out to be filled, she added helplessly, "Except to – to give you back your ring, of course."

His glance went to her hand then, and he said rather stonily, "You're not wearing my ring."

"I never wore it. Not even when I – I had the right to. Now I – have no right." But instinctively her hand went to her breast for a moment.

187

She had forgotten that he was used to interpreting the smallest gesture on the stage and that his artistic observation never failed him. He moved so quickly that he was beside her in an instant and, before she could make the smallest movement of dissent, he had slipped his fingers under the chain and lifted the ring from its hiding place.

It lay there, sparkling in the palm of his hand, still warm from its contact with her.

"Why were you wearing it, Mary?" The harshness had gone out of his voice, but she could not raise her eyes to look at him. She could only stare down at the ring lying in the palm of that strong, sensitive hand.

"I meant to give it back," she whispered. "I did – truly. I just wanted to keep it for – for a little while longer."

"Why, dear? Why did you want to keep it?"

The unexpected endearment took her last ounce of self-control away. She shook her head wordlessly. And as she did so history repeated itself in the most extraordinary way. A tear dropped on his hand, just as it had all that time ago in the concert hall, when she thought he was angry with her. It lay there beside the diamond, like some absurd little poor relation of the other sparkling drop.

"Don't cry," he said softly. "Don't cry, my dear one. I'm not worth it."

"But you are – you are!" she exclaimed despairingly. "That's just it. You're everything – to me. The great star – the wonderful artist, the man I lo-" She stopped suddenly, her hand against her lips.

"Say that again," he said urgently, taking her in his arms and holding her close.

"About the great star and the wonderful artist?" She was suddenly smiling rather tremulously.

"No, the other bit. The phrase you didn't finish."

"The man I love," said Mary slowly, savouring every syllable, and she reached up and kissed him. "I love you, Nicholas. However unworthy and stupid and unkind I may have been –"

"Don't say such things!" he interrupted almost angrily. "I won't have anyone say such things of the woman I love. They're not true, anyway – any more than those absurd, self-pitying phrases in that odious letter of mine were true."

"Some of them were," she murmured.

"None of them," he insisted. "When I received *your* letter –"

"Oh, Nicholas! you did get it, then?"

"But only yesterday, tragically late. And every dear and warm and generous sentence in it was a reproach to me. So utterly different from the way I wrote to you. And when you were ill, too! though I didn't know that. How can you ever forgive me?"

"Very easily. If you can forgive me too."

"Come, darling, and sit beside me." He drew her down on to a sofa. Then he deliberately unfastened the chain round her neck and released the ring. "May I put it where it really belongs?" He took her left hand lightly in his.

"If you're sure – if you're absolutely sure –"

"Of what, my dear?"

"That you can trust me to be generous and sensible and understanding, and never, never, never to be jealous and unreasonable again."

"It isn't I who needs to be reassured, Mary." He slipped the ring on her finger and put her hand to his lips. "Are *you* sure that you want a temperamental, unpredictable opera singer for a husband?"

"I want you," Mary said. "That's all. It's quite simple.

Like all great truths."

"I don't deserve it," he said humbly. "At least, I don't think I do," and he smiled at her with that sudden quirk of humour which had first endeared him to her.

"Of course you do," she insisted. "Or if not, I don't deserve my happiness either. For we've both made mistakes, Nicholas dear, and both have something to forgive. Let the reproaches and the remorse cancel out each other."

"Which is a way of saying – let the past bury the past," he said, smiling as he took her in his arms again. "It's the future that matters, and the future is ours, Mary – all of it."

Then he looked beyond her with an expression of extraordinary tranquillity, and in that moment she was nearly sure that he said a final good-bye to his unhappy past – *senza rancor*.